Why would he keep to the shadows and never be seen? Never venture outside?

The wind continued to buffet them. Rain slanted under the awning. Noah seemed disinclined to leave. Angel certainly didn't want to. Not with her attacker still lurking out there. But someone had to move. Or speak. Or act.

A second headlight sliced through the alley.

The split-second shot of Noah's profile made the breath in Angel's lungs stall.

The word *stunning* sprang to mind, followed by *sexy* and *sensual*. Tall, dark-haired.

Her eyes moved upward to the shadow that still managed to blot out most of his face. "I saw you, Noah, just for a second, and you're gorgeous. Why on earth…?"

It was all she got out. This time it was Noah who moved, Noah who framed her face with his hands to hold her still. Noah who murmured a regretful, "I'm going to pay for this…" And then he crushed his mouth onto hers.

25 years of INTRIGUE

Dear Harlequin Intrigue Reader,

In honor of two very special events, the Harlequin Intrigue editorial team has planned exceptional promotions to celebrate throughout 2009. To kick off the year, we're celebrating Harlequin Books' 60th Diamond Anniversary with DIAMONDS AND DADDIES, an exciting four-book miniseries featuring protective dads and their extraordinary proposals to four very lucky women. Rita Herron launches the series with *Platinum Cowboy* next month.

Later in the year Harlequin Intrigue celebrates its own 25th anniversary. To mark the event we've asked reader favorites to return with their most popular series.

• Debra Webb has created a new COLBY AGENCY trilogy. This time out, Victoria Colby-Camp will need to enlist the help of her entire staff of agents for her own family crisis.

• You can return to 43 LIGHT STREET with Rebecca York and join Caroline Burnes on another crime-solving mission with Familiar the Black Cat Detective.

• Next stop: WHITEHORSE, MONTANA with B.J. Daniels for more Big Sky mysteries with a new family. Meet the Corbetts—Shane, Jud, Dalton, Lantry and Russell.

Because we know our readers love following trace evidence, we've created the new continuity KENNER COUNTY CRIME UNIT. Whether collecting evidence or tracking down leads, lawmen and investigators have more than their jobs on the line, because the real mystery is one of the heart. Pick up *Secrets in Four Corners* by Debra Webb this month, and don't miss any one of the terrific stories to follow in this series.

And that's just a small selection of what we have planned to thank our readers.

We'd love to hear from you, and hope you enjoy all of our special promotions this year.

Happy reading, and happy anniversary, Harlequin Books!

Sincerely,

Denise Zaza
Senior Editor
Harlequin Intrigue

JENNA RYAN

A VOICE IN THE DARK

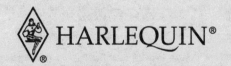

HARLEQUIN®

TORONTO • NEW YORK • LONDON
AMSTERDAM • PARIS • SYDNEY • HAMBURG
STOCKHOLM • ATHENS • TOKYO • MILAN • MADRID
PRAGUE • WARSAW • BUDAPEST • AUCKLAND

To Merlyn.
Keep fighting, sweetheart.
Win or lose, we'll always love you.

Recycling programs
for this product may
not exist in your area.

ISBN-13: 978-0-373-88885-6
ISBN-10:   0-373-88885-6

A VOICE IN THE DARK

Copyright © 2009 by Jacqueline Goff

www.eHarlequin.com

Printed in U.S.A.

ABOUT THE AUTHOR

Jenna Ryan loves creating dark-haired heroes, heroines with strength and good murder mysteries. Ever since she was young, she has had an extremely active imagination. She considered various careers over the years and dabbled in several of them, until the day her sister Kathy suggested she put her imagination to work and write a book. She enjoys working with intriguing characters and feels she is at her best writing romantic suspense. When people ask her how she writes, she tells them, "By instinct." Clearly it's worked, since she's received numerous awards from *Romantic Times BOOKreviews*. She lives in Canada and travels as much as she can when she's not writing.

Books by Jenna Ryan

HARLEQUIN INTRIGUE

88—CAST IN WAX
99—SUSPENDED ANIMATION
118—CLOAK AND DAGGER
138—CARNIVAL
145—SOUTHERN CROSS
173—MASQUERADE
189—ILLUSIONS
205—PUPPETS
221—BITTERSWEET LEGACY
239—THE VISITOR
251—MIDNIGHT MASQUE
265—WHEN NIGHT FALLS
364—BELLADONNA
393—SWEET REVENGE
450—THE WOMAN IN BLACK
488—THE ARMS OF THE LAW
543—THE STROKE OF MIDNIGHT

816—EDEN'S SHADOW
884—CHRISTMAS RANSOM
922—DREAM WEAVER
972—COLD CASE COWBOY
1027—MISTLETOE
    AND MURDER
1078—DANGEROUSLY
    ATTRACTIVE
1111—A VOICE IN THE DARK

CAST OF CHARACTERS

Angel Carter—FBI agent assigned to the Penny Killer investigation. She has worked with Noah for more than a year—but has never seen him.

Noah Graydon—A criminal profiler for the FBI, Noah lives in a world of shadows and mystery.

Liz Thomas—Angel's partner has a secret that interferes with their current investigation.

Joe Thomas—The forensic pathologist is one of only a very few people who have seen Noah in the past five years.

Graeme Thomas—He is Joe's brother. Since the Penny Killer's murders began, his behavior has altered dramatically.

Paul Reuben—A dogged reporter who knows far more than he should about the Penny Killer.

Brian Pinkeney—A federal agent with a grudge against Noah.

Pete Peloni—He owns a restaurant in Little Italy, and has a past he prefers to hide.

Prologue

"Who are you?" The man on the dock frowned. "You said it was urgent. You told me…" His voice flattened. "You lied."

"I did. But you love, so you believed. You were vulnerable. That's how I succeed. Love is joy. It's also pain. Which emotion we experience depends on the person we love."

A cruel north wind blasted the man from behind. His muscles tightened beneath his overcoat. His hand crept toward his pocket.

The person opposite smiled. "There's no point trying to be subtle. I can see you have a gun."

The man's fingers balled.

"You know, for such an educated man, you strike me as rather stupid. Still, I don't really expect you or anyone to understand. It doesn't work that way in my case."

A knife blade appeared out of nowhere to press against the man's throat. He made a choking sound and froze.

"Maybe not quite so stupid after all. But an unfortunate victim just the same."

"Why are you doing this?" the man whispered. "Can't I at least know that?"

"I already told you. Love is pain."

"Which you're going to inflict."

"Unfortunately."

Before the man could react, the knife shifted. The blade slashed.

Blood spurted, a steaming red fountain of it.

The man jolted and clawed. He tried to grab the knife, as if that would help. He staggered forward in an attempt to run.

But he was dead, and he knew it, even if he didn't know why.

When the job was done, the man's killer stood back. A measure of sorrow crept in and, yes, pity. But no second thought. No regrets.

The time for waiting was over.

It had begun. Again.

Chapter One

A dockyard in Boston

Wind whipped the rain-soaked body of the forty-something male who lay prostrate on the pavement. Two pennies, one shiny, one dull, sat on his closed eyelids. Even so, FBI agent Angel Carter thought he looked shocked, as if he couldn't believe he was dead.

Behind her, a Boston police officer made notes and muttered. About the federal presence, Angel imagined. Or maybe he didn't like the traditional "time of death" pool taking place around him.

"Four hours," one of the patrols said.

"It's forty degrees," another argued. "Factor in the wind chill and we're talking thirty or less. The guy's stiff and blue. I'll go under three."

Their voices swirled around Angel's head like the stinging pellets of rain. She studied the corpse and waited patiently for the official pronouncement of death.

At length, the medical examiner stripped off his gloves and blew on his hands. "Someone sliced him up real good, Angel." He pointed. "Opened the carotid artery, which is why you'll find a diluted stream of blood from the dock halfway to your place. Guy's big and well built. Probably put up a fight, but only with one hand. He was trying to stem the blood flow with the other."

One of the uniforms leaned in. "How long d'you figure, Doc? I'm in for three and a half hours."

"Joe's the one who puts the stamp on the time of death," Angel reminded him.

"I only confirm that he is in fact dead." The medical examiner signaled the ambulance attendants. "And this one definitely is. Has been since a minute or two after the knife sliced his neck."

Angel had trained herself long ago not to let a victim's facial expression affect her. Easier to focus on the wounds.

As the ME left, Angel's eyes followed the gash on the victim's neck. "It's a jagged slash. Either the killer had an unsteady hand or the victim was struggling. Second thing makes more sense."

Uninterested, the uniform moved off. Another pair of boots sloshed in. The woman wearing them hunkered down. "The victim's name is Lionel Foret. Forty-two years old. Officially, he lived in Boston, but his work appears to have taken him between here and DC."

"Government?"

"So his soggy credentials say. State Department. Bergman might know more by the time we check in."

"He has the look of a politician. Or a lawyer. Whatever he is, Bergman barked at me to get down here, and in the year and a half I've known him, he's never barked."

"Ditto." Liz fingered the man's coat. "His clothes say major money, but with the exception of his driver's license and a few credit cards, his wallet's empty. My guess is he was rolled by a junkie."

The skin on Angel's neck tingled, as if an army of invisible ants were marching across it. She glanced behind her. "Do you feel something, Liz?"

"Other than waterlogged?"

"I think we're being watched."

FBI agent Elizabeth Thomas blew out a steamy breath. "Any thief desperate enough to slice a guy in this weather won't be hanging around to observe the cleanup crew. He's long gone and probably high as Franklin's kite by now. Which is why we'll nail him before first light."

"If the perp's an addict."

"Okay, it's an assumption, but my money's on the easy answer this time."

Sensation, like a finger stroked across the back of her neck, sent a shiver of reaction down Angel's spine. "Okay, this is way too weird." She whipped her head around, but saw only shadows behind the fish processing plant. "Someone's back there."

Liz rose with her. "I promise you, Angel, there's no one. We told the cops to secure the area, and they did. All shadows duly checked, all boxes on the list ticked empty." She nudged her partner's high-heeled boot with her toe. "Maybe your brain's starting to freeze. You're not exactly dressed for this weather."

"I was at a play when Bergman called."

"Lucky you. I'd just settled my toddler into bed and was thinking about streaking my hair for the holidays. Can you believe Thanksgiving's only three weeks away?" She squinted at the threatening sky. "It seems like summer just ended."

"Apparently you turned Rip Van Winkle and slept through last week's blizzard."

"That was a freak storm."

"That was six inches of snow the last week of October. Normal for Juneau, but in Boston I expected a glorious New England fall, up to and hopefully through Thanksgiving. Didn't get it last year, and so far this one's a rerun."

"Write to the Tourist Bureau. They print the brochures." Liz ran her fingers through her short blond hair. "Was the play good?"

"The first act was."

Although she scanned and rescanned the darkness, nothing moved except the rain, currently being driven sideways by a gale-force wind that gusted in hard from the water.

And still the sensation persisted, a featherlight

breath on her face, then along the line of her cheek to her throat.

Liz nudged her again. "We need to get inside. You might have grown up in Alaska, but I'm a Corpus Christi girl and highly susceptible to wet rot. I swear on my nine years of federal service, there's no one and nothing back there."

One final hint of warm, and suddenly it was only the wind on her cheeks.

Angel shook her head. "Weird," she murmured one last time. But she had to admit as the victim's body was prepped for removal, that despite the unsettling aspect, the sensation had felt strangely like a caress.

Completely sensual, and in an instant, completely gone.

HE WATCHED HER from the narrow walkway that split the old processing plant in two. She'd sensed him. He'd seen it in the way her eyes cruised the shadows, as if she'd known more than rats and cockroaches lurked within them.

Suspicion had come first, followed by speculation. Then, when the feeling persisted, impatience.

In unguarded moments, Angel Carter wore her emotions on her face, her incredibly beautiful face. Those same emotions added an element of intrigue to her already exotic features...

And he was thinking like a man obsessed.

Still, he didn't move, didn't let his gaze waver.

Didn't mean he missed the body at her feet, but he'd seen that already, before she'd arrived.

"Someone's back there, Liz…"

He heard the determination now, and his lips curved. He should go, leave her with partner and corpse, let her draw her conclusions and see where they led.

Icy rain slid along his neck beneath his upturned collar. The man in black. The man who lived in the dark. A phantom. That's how people described him. He didn't care. Phantoms could slip in and out undetected.

Except, apparently, by an Angel.

When her partner set a hand on her arm, he knew it was time to vanish. He'd done what he'd come to do. Now it was her turn.

The shadows shifted as the ambulance arrived. He allowed himself one last look, then disappeared into the heart of them.

Chapter Two

The hands of the clock ticked slowly toward 2:00 a.m. Angel had spoken to her boss three times since viewing the body and his sniveling assistant twice. This time she had a somewhat different number in mind.

She was positioning her thumb over the seventh digit when the head of forensic pathology pushed through the lab door. His smile was automatic, his chuckle a welcome sound in the sterile grid of hospital corridors.

"He won't mind," Joe Thomas assured her. "Two, four, six o'clock. Time of day or night is irrelevant to Noah Graydon. As you should know after eighteen months of back-and-forth phone conversations."

Angel's own smile blossomed. "Good to hear, Dr. T, but in actual fact, I was calling my mother. And after almost thirty years of close association, I can promise you time means a great deal to her. More than her new Harley, in fact."

"Amazing woman." Joe used a blue checked handkerchief to polish his glasses. "She crunches numbers in Alaska for the better part of four decades, then meets a long distance trucker and decides to go off and live the life."

"Everyone should live the life." Angel closed her phone, met his brown eyes. "Not sure about the Harley yet, but I'm always open to new. Why did you think I was calling Noah?"

"Come on, Angel, I've met Bergman's snotty assistant. The voice of reason would be a welcome change after that. Unfortunately, in terms of your latest murder victim, I'm leaning toward a mugging gone awry."

"Been talking to your wife, huh?"

"Yes, I have, and yes, the word junkie came up, but she's only trying to keep things simple after that nightmare of a childnapping case you two were involved in."

Angel dropped the cell phone into her coat pocket. "So what's the deal with Foret?"

Joe crooked a finger. "Come into my parlor, pretty fly, and I'll show you."

"Great, I get to see a naked dead man on an empty stomach. Missed dinner," she explained, "along with the ending to the play."

"Who was the unlucky guy?"

She shed her coat, grinned. "A podiatrist your wife and my so-called friend introduced me to last week. He looks, talks and acts like a department store mannequin. He has polished skin, Joe, right down to the cleft in his chin. He also has an icky foot fetish which I'll be kind and not go into. Now fess up. Why did you think I was calling Noah?"

He pinched her chin before snapping on a pair of medical gloves. "Cat with a fish, Angel, that's you. Okay, I thought that because it's what you do when you're feeling edgy, and Liz told me about the shadow thing tonight. You thought someone was watching you."

Unperturbed, Angel circled the examining table. "Watching all of us, Doc. I'm not totally paranoid."

"Just ultra sensitive to dark shadows. And bats."

"Some people would call the shadow part intuitive."

"Was anyone lurking?"

"Not that I saw, but shadows shift, and anyone in them would know how to move fast. I'm not saying there's a deep dark plot involved here, but I'm not thinking junkie either. The pennies on Foret's eyelids," she elaborated at Joe's slight frown. "It's too old-world for someone who's desperate."

"Are you thinking hired hit?"

"Could be. Foret worked for the State Department—that's all the information Bergman has or is giving us right now—but I'm guessing he was high level. He was also on that dock for a reason. We'll start there."

"Well, deep breath, stomach muscles tight, let's have a look at Mr. Foret's wounds."

The better part of an hour crawled by, leaving in its wake the eerie sense of mortality that struck her from time to time.

As Joe's colleague had suggested, it was the slash to Foret's carotid artery that had done the job. He'd bled out swiftly with little time to react and only one hand with which to defend himself. Most of the scoring was on his throat and neck, but there was also a nick on his collarbone and a shallow scrape on the back of his hand.

"There's possible blood and or skin under the fingernails of his left hand," Joe noted. "I'll have those things plus the contents of his stomach analyzed and on your desk by noon."

"Sunday dinner should be fun."

Joe blinked at her through his wire-rimmed glasses. "Is it Sunday already?"

"Between home, work and the Victim's Support Center, you and Liz work way too hard." Angel moved away from the table, shook the smell of death from her hair and arms. "You should take a cruise."

"We thought about it, but I get seasick."

She couldn't resist a laugh. The man dissected dead bodies, but a few ocean swells did him in. The human mind fascinated.

She heard a thump. The door to the examining room swung open, and a second Dr. Thomas squished in.

"Liz called," he explained before his brother

could ask. "There's a liver coming in from Atlanta. The patient's being prepped for transplant surgery, so I decided to drop in and thaw my nimble fingers. Dead guy on the table aside, have any new donors been wheeled in tonight?"

Twisted amusement rose in Angel's throat. "Foret's are the only body parts in the vicinity, Graeme, so put your eyes back in their sockets, go upstairs and scrub."

Several inches taller and a great deal more handsome than his comfortable-looking older brother, Graeme Thomas was nevertheless an inherently nice guy. Didn't mean he couldn't flirt with the best of them. "You talk so sweet, Angel." Flashing a grin, he set his cheek next to hers from behind, wrapped his arms around her waist and swayed. "Sure you won't marry me?"

"That would make me what? Wife number four?"

"It's my lucky number. Come on, what do you say? You, me, Elvis, a neon chapel? I'll even rent us a pink Cadillac."

She smiled and patted his exposed cheek. "Really tempted, but I'll settle for dinner and a DVD."

"Topped off by a chat with Noah Graydon?"

"Not you, too." She sighed out a breath, disentangled and turned. "Noah's a friend, okay? On the invisible side, but if people can connect through the Internet, then the phone should be a no-brainer."

"I guess." But he caught her hand. "The Vegas offer stands. You get tired of a voice on the phone, you know where I'll be."

"Yeah, up to your elbows in body parts. I'll hold tight to that image. Send the report over when you get it, Joe. I'm going to try for—" she brought her watch into focus "—whoa, four straight hours of alone time. Tell Liz I'll finish the prelims, and she should go ahead and streak her hair."

"Are all women anal with their priorities?" Graeme wondered aloud.

Angel pulled on her gloves, worked the fingers down. "No more so than men with their HD TVs and game-day rituals. Good luck in surgery, Graeme."

Her boot heels echoed in the empty corridor outside. Swinging her coat on, she murmured, "It's like being the last live cell in a dead body. No way could I do your job, Dr. T."

Still, as her newly emancipated mother liked to say, life tossed what it tossed. Go with it or go crazy.

At twenty-nine, Angel didn't think life had tossed all that much her way yet. But three girl-friends and a messy divorce later, her father had done his level best to drive his first wife crazy. Thankfully, poetic justice had intervened. He'd wound up with a shrew for a second wife along with the proverbial stepchild from hell. As Angel saw it, occasionally life and fate got together and tossed a very satisfying fair ball into the mix.

Deep in the pocket of her black coat, her cell phone began to hum. At three-something in the morning, the news wasn't likely to be good, but ever the optimist, she pulled it out.

The number on the screen brought a smile to her lips, even if it didn't surprise. For all his solitary ways, the man knew everything, often before anyone else in the department.

She greeted him with an amused, "Well, hi there, tall, dark and mysterious. What's got you up so late on a Saturday night?"

"Mostly the thought of you being up so late on a Saturday night."

Noah Graydon's voice flowed through her veins like honey laced with dark rum. She'd been intrigued by him since their first conversation, a year and a half ago. Today, she was as much entranced as intrigued. Unfortunately, she was also inured, or heading that way.

Noah was a man of darkness, a voice in the night. For reasons she had yet to determine, he preferred to exist in a world of shadow and half-light. No one saw him except Joe. And no one who knew him, if indeed anyone in the Boston office did, would talk about his predilection for solitude.

And so their entire relationship had evolved over the phone. Didn't make him a stranger exactly, but if she'd been the cat Joe had labeled her, curiosity would have killed her several lifetimes ago.

Smiling, even though she knew where their conversation would ultimately wind up, Angel pushed the elevator call button, then bumped her shoulder lightly against the wall while she waited.

"I'm at the path lab and creeped out, Noah. Say something pretty so I can erase the picture of dead body parts that are whizzing through my brain."

"Bed of roses."

She set her head on the wall. "Been listening to Bon Jovi, huh?"

"That's why the Boston office snapped you up, Angel. You're all about extrapolation. Okay, pretty. Close your eyes and imagine the Cape. Turning leaves and bonfires. Think cold nights, a walk in the woods and a glass of wine waiting when you return."

A more tranquil smile curved her lips. "You have a truly amazing voice, Graydon. I swear I can smell those leaves burning." The elevator doors slid open, and she glanced inside. "Yuck. Empty gurney with rumpled sheets." She sidestepped it as she entered.

His low chuckle might have brought back the Cape if she hadn't recalled the unholy hour. A clunk of gears preceded the elevator's arduous upward climb.

"I hear you've got a body," he remarked.

"We do, and I've just come from a close encounter with it. It's big, pale and hairless, a bit like that enormous baby the drunk stork delivered to the wrong people in the Bugs Bunny cartoon."

"Well, there's a picture. Thanks for that, Angel."

"Welcome. Do you know what Foret's story is?"

"He's got ties to the White House."

"Figured as much. Just please don't tell me he's related to someone who's going to make my life hell until his murder's solved."

"He's a lawyer."

"Explains the eight-hundred-dollar suit."

"Attached to the State Department."

"Saw the credentials. Tell me what I didn't see, or probably wouldn't know."

"He's close personal friends with the current Secretary of State."

At last, the inevitable X factor reared its head. "Oh, good. That means there'll be pressure to solve and close fast. Bergman can't be aware of the last thing, Noah, or instead of sniveling, his assistant would be apoplectic. Is there any whisper about a dockyard rendezvous?"

"Give me time, Angel. I just dug up the Secretary of State connection. Any theories yet?"

Angel caught herself stroking the bottom of her cell phone and gave her fingers a speculative look.

"Only that I don't think he was rolled by someone hungry for a fix. It's true, any cash he had in his wallet was gone, but he was still wearing his platinum Tag Heuer watch, diamond tiepin and ring. Signet, not wedding. So either the killer was dumb as well as desperate, or the money was taken to make Foret's death look like a really bad mugging. "

"How did you read the pennies on his eyes?"

"I've heard of similar cases."

"Yeah?"

"Three times last year. Once in Boston, twice in New York. All of the murders had gangland connections. One gang, three killers."

"This isn't gang-related."

It wouldn't be, she thought. Far too simple. "And you know that because?"

"Victim doesn't fit the profile."

"Yes, well, Noah, it's late and I'm tired, and it was really cold on that dock. I wasn't thinking profile so much as get him to Joe and find the largest possible coffee."

Another chuckle reached her. It almost reached into her. "Don't turn diva on me, Angel. It wasn't a criticism. You only came to Boston eighteen months ago. You can't know what I do."

Eighteen months, and some odd number of days. Angel started to lean a hip on the gurney, but spied the soiled undersheet and opted for the elevator rail instead. "Waiting, Graydon. What exactly is it you know?"

"This isn't an isolated murder." Softly said, but a chill chased itself along her spine.

"Definitely do not like the sound of that. Are we talking serial killing?"

"I'd say so."

Frustration crept in as the elevator ground to a halt. "How can you think that already? Have you been talking to Joe?"

"I don't have to talk to Joe."

"Then how…?"

"Look for a note."

Again, the words were softly uttered; however, far from diminishing their impact, Noah's tone gave them a punch that silenced Angel's automatic protest.

"What kind of note?" she asked instead.

"A cryptic one. This killer's looking to be understood, but only by the cleverest of the clever."

She pictured him leaning forward in his chair, staring at the rain-smeared city lights outside his window.

"It'll be small," he continued. "Ordinary, like a tossed off scrap of paper. But it will be there. Look hard enough, and you'll find it."

Her resistance dissolved. "You're the best criminal profiler in the business, Graydon. I trust you more than anyone I know. So I'll look. And if there's a note, I'll find it. Bergman…"

"Doesn't need to know about my involvement in this case."

His statement surprised her into stopping halfway across the reception area. "Say that again? Don't tell my boss why I'm doing what I'm doing?"

"It wouldn't be the first time you've withheld, Angel. This one's for me. Call it a personal favor."

She responded to the admissions nurse's wave with an absent smile. Something stirred deep inside, but she was fairly certain it had nothing to do with correct procedure and everything to do with an overwhelming resurgence of curiosity.

"Cat with a fish," she echoed.

"Is that a yes?"

The obvious question clawed at her throat, but she swallowed it and looked out into the inky darkness. "You're a fascinating man, Noah Graydon. I respect you, I like you, and God knows I owe you. So if more mystery's what you want, I'm in. For your sake and Lionel Foret's, it's a yes."

INSIDE HIS SPARSELY FURNISHED North Bay loft, Noah propped a bare foot on the windowsill and sipped hot coffee.

He didn't bother to rouse himself when he heard the freight elevator clunk past the twelfth floor. He lived alone on thirteen, had since the only other person brave enough to overcome the eighteenth-century ghost story that was part and parcel of the building's charm had taken a header out a rear window into a row of trashcans below.

The elevator gate rattled up. Ten seconds later, he heard a knuckle rap, and the door creaked open.

"It's me, Noah. You feel like company?"

Noah rested his head on the chair back. "If I didn't, would you go away?"

"Probably not." Joe came in, collided with a metal stand next to the door and swore. "Friggin' vampire lighting. Don't you even want to see where you live?"

Noah smiled a little. "Did you come here to

bitch about my furniture or to pass along useable information?"

"The second thing, but I swear, some day the first's gonna cripple me. I smell coffee."

"Machine's still next to the fridge."

"That would be the big black box at ten o'clock, right?"

Noah kept his eyes on the flickering city lights. "What's the news, Joe?"

"I'll—ouch—preface it by reminding you that I'm not supposed to be talking about this."

"Pretend you've made the spiel. Why did Bergman give Foret to Angel and Liz?"

"Because they're good not working for you?"

Noah merely turned his head to stare.

His friend released an audible breath. "Fine, he did it because of you. We might think all pen pushers are jackasses, but one or two of them actually have a brain. Liz and Angel *are* good, but official or not, you're the prize Bergman's after. Your boss wants you to back off this one—word's already out on that—so Bergman had to go for your Achilles' heel. Namely, Angel Carter."

Noah turned back to his view. "So far, she can tell me as much or more than I can tell her."

"What are you—ouch—okay, you moved that table, right?" Joe stopped to rub his shin. "What's going on in your head about Foret's death?"

"If you know what my boss is up to, you already know what's going on."

"You think it's that guy again, don't you, the one who did that string of murders that started seven years ago?"

"Eight."

"We'll call that an affirmative. Why?"

Noah propped his other foot up. "You did Foret's autopsy. You tell me."

"Team's still running the results, but from the prelim, I'd say the wounds are fairly consistent. Still, a lot of murderers use knives. I think you're reaching if your goal is to resurrect a serial killer who's been off the map for half a decade."

"We'll see."

Joe came to perch on the ledge. "Let's get personal, shall we? How're you doing these days? I cook a mean pot roast, and Liz's angel food cakes are as divine as their name implies. Break down and have dinner with us. Liz is dying to meet you, and Jaynie turned four last Friday. We'll have a second birthday party. You can give her money to buy new shoes."

Noah smiled. "Your four-year-old likes shoes?"

"She takes after her adopted aunt. Angel loves shoes more than life. Liz only loves them more than paying bills." Leaning forward, he tapped Noah's knee. "We'll eat by candlelight, tell the girls you're a vampire with a soul, or whatever the deal was for that Buffy character. They'll be mesmerized."

Noah let his head fall back on the chair. "Thanks just the same."

Joe emitted a sound of frustrated acceptance. "It isn't healthy, you know, how you live—or don't live as the case may be."

"My life, my business, Dr. Thomas."

"Don't Dr. Thomas me. I'll bet the house that you've seen Angel live and in person without her having a clue she's been observed. The least you could do is return the favor."

Okay, now that *was* too personal. Noah shot him a look that had Joe's mouth ratcheting closed.

"Yeah, fine, got it. Back off or take off. But I have to tell you, she's pretty spectacular up close."

"I've seen her, Joe."

"Nuh-uh, not up close, you haven't, and animated. I'll take a page out of Graeme's book and wax poetic for a moment, because she's—well, beautiful." He used his hands. "Hair the color of Mayan coffee, miles of it, gorgeous hazel eyes, legs that go from here to my waist and incredible skin. Of course, being married, I'm not supposed to notice things like that, and I know better than to say any of them around my wife, but truth's truth, and you're missing the boat where Angel's concerned, because I promise you, she's interested, even if you are just a disembodied voice in the night... Now you really are going to tell me to shove off, aren't you, so end of speech. What say we work on our chess game? I believe it's my move."

Joe's move, yes, but not his game to play. Not his risk to take.

Not his dragon to slay.

Draining his mug, Noah said, "She's better off out of it. She doesn't need my demons added to her own."

"If you mean her daddy dearest, she doesn't mourn the loss. Some fathers are great—no names, please. Others are total jackasses. You got the cream of the crop in that regard. Angel lucked out physically." Joe walked to the sofa, hesitated, then blurted an impatient, "You're not a monster, you know."

Noah couldn't help it, he laughed. "Man, do all pathologists take drama as a minor in college?" He dropped his feet. "I'll meet her when I meet her, okay? Right now, Foret's the focus. Mine and hers. And your king's in serious trouble."

"Nothing new there." Joe waited until they were seated on opposite sides of the board before meeting Noah's stare. "You really think it's him, don't you? The guy who went on that three-year killing spree, then suddenly stopped."

"Yeah, I do."

"Even though the evidence in some of those cases was dicey."

"Still a yes."

His friend's hand trembled visibly. "Noah, Liz…"

"Won't die, okay?" Noah held his gaze without a flicker. "Neither will Angel."

"A statement you hope is true, but can't be sure

of—unless that patch you wear shoots psychic vibrations directly into your brain."

Noah didn't respond, merely rested his forearms on his knees and regarded the chessboard. He spoke to more than his friend when he said softly, "Your move."

Chapter Three

"Okay, so Lionel Foret was what? A Munster wannabe?" Liz stomped her feet on the porch of what was possibly the most decrepit house in Boston. In front of her, Angel rattled an old-fashioned key in the rusted-out lock.

They'd already gone through Foret's Boston apartment, top to bottom, and found nothing except a million newspapers, enough fast-food containers to fill a city Dumpster and one very fat canary which Foret's mother, currently en route from Virginia, was planning to take home.

"You heard his mom." Angel used her shoulder on the stuck door. "Lionel wanted to fix and flip this place. He spent as much time here as he did in his apartment. The other third of his life unfolded in Washington."

"We've got people checking the DC condo, right?"

"Yeah, and his buddy the Secretary is all over them. Bergman's going down to talk to the man live and in person."

"Better him than us… Can I help you push?"

"Nope." Angel braced, gave a hard shove—and almost wound up flat on her face in the foyer as the engorged wood gave. "Got it."

She shone her flashlight over the wall. "I smell old dust, fresh paint and foo yung. What a combo." Locating the switch, she flipped it up. "Well, that made a world of difference. One twenty-five watt bulb spread over how many hundreds of junk-filled square feet? Still, the foo yung and paint say he's been here recently." She pivoted in a slow circle. "Wow—this is great."

"It's cold, it stinks, and it's probably crawling with bugs." Liz inspected the sagging ceiling. "Bergman's a supreme ass for sticking us with this job while he takes a cushy flight to Washington."

Angel gave her shoulder a tap with the flashlight. "Better him than us, remember? Come on, Liz, where's your sense of adventure? This is the Munster house. Scratch fixing and flipping. Foret should have added costumed workers to the cobwebs and marketed it as a hotel."

"You've got to be joking."

"People said that about ice hotels, and look what happened there. Do you want up or down?"

"Kitchen'll be down. I'll go up. Reinforcements are coming, right?"

"A team of four. Two rookies."

"Perfect, they can do the bathrooms." She snagged the back of Angel's jacket. "Be careful."

"Always am. Watch out for rats on the stairs."

"Like I could miss them," her friend muttered. "Place like this, they'll be as big as wolves."

"Werewolves," Angel corrected and laughed when Liz flung a small chunk of plaster at her.

Not that she enjoyed mold and mildew, but calling it the Munster house kept her on the upside of the fantasy. Because, God knew, on the down, she'd be envisioning bats by now. Big ones, grinning like little ghouls, and walking awkwardly as bats tended to do, across the floor.

Her cell phone rang while she was forging a path toward the back of the house. By way of a greeting, she demanded, "Question, Noah, did Eddie's pet Fang live under the house or under the stairs?"

"Is this a riddle, Angel, or do you always do hallucinogenic drugs at 11:00 a.m. on a Monday?" But he sounded halfway amused, which helped with the bat phobia.

Angel's foot slid off a section of crumbled wall. "Bergman gave us the victim's Mockingbird Lane fixer. Wasn't that sweet? The lights are Edison originals, and if there's such a thing as a furnace, I can't believe it'd work." She set a hand on the chair rail for balance. "There was no note in his downtown apartment. Liz and I spent hours yesterday searching. We had a hacker go through his Blackberry and laptop. Nothing. And both of his briefcases came up empty. If he was meeting someone on the dock, he kept the date, time and identity in his head. We have no witnesses so far and very few other clues. Even Joe doesn't have anything for us yet. I'm thinking slow slog here."

"Keep looking."

"That's my job—oh, yuck, something squished under my boot." She wouldn't look, she promised herself. Hearing a thud, she glanced at the massive staircase. "Spooky," she decided, then strained to see around a peeling column, "Yellow walls ahead. Could be Foret was trying to force-feed sunshine into the place."

"You're there for evidence, not ambience."

"Uh-huh. And you're where right now? Fifty bucks says it's some place warm, dry and mildew-free. Oh thank God, the squishy stuff was only a tube of caulking. Foret's mother told us he slept here most of last week. She's a police dispatcher in Virginia, used to be a beat cop." A loose wire twined around Angel's ankle and she had to crouch to dislodge it. "Her boyfriend's driving her up this week. I gather she's terrified of flying."

"Yeah, I read the back files. Joy Foret Smith's first husband was a pilot for a major airline. He had a heart attack between Boston and Jacksonville. Died in the cockpit. She took a leave of absence afterward, for her nerves. Her second husband ran an Internet business. A blood clot got him while they were on vacation at Martha's Vineyard. Word is she's sworn off marriage and is currently living with a cop because she's decided it's no more dangerous than any other occupation."

Angel found herself smiling—and surprisingly already standing on the kitchen threshold.

She located the overhead switch, but again, the light was virtually nonexistent. "You're a wonderful distraction, Graydon. Okay, so I'm in the kitchen. I see three containers of Chinese food on a slopey surface that's probably a counter. He's got his used paint rollers wrapped in plastic, and the big goodies, hopefully appliances, draped with tarps. Lily'd love this place."

"Lily?"

"Munster." She ran her flashlight into the corners. "You own a TV, right?"

"Search, Angel."

"I can do that and talk at the same time. Hang on, I'm putting you on speaker." Depressing the button, she set the phone next to a disposable cup.

Wind whistled through the ill-fitting rear door. The bigger gusts shifted the floor dust and caused the rafters to moan.

Angel's sharp eyes spied the end of a sleeping bag behind the rickety island. Pulling off her cap and gloves, she shook her hair loose. "Looks like Foret slept in the kitchen. I have to say, this area's a lot better than the entry hall—except for the yellow walls. Too canary-like. If he was trying for French country, which he shouldn't be in a pre-Revolution house, he missed by a mile."

"French farmers don't like canaries?"

She sighed in the direction of the counter. "Do you have even a drop of European blood in your veins?"

She heard the smile in his voice when he replied. "I happen to know you're one hundred percent American, Angel. Three generations worth."

"Ah, but go back to gen four, and we're talking major global mix. One of my great-grandmothers came from Africa. The other was born in Fiji. My mother's paternal grandfather was a Brit and the maternal one a potpourri—Italian, Romanian and Norwegian."

"You missed the Argentine connection."

She narrowed her eyes at the phone. "I swear to God, Graydon, if you can tell me what color bra I'm wearing, I'm cutting you off right now."

"I'll go with white and lacy."

Lips twitching, she resumed her search. "Not going to react, because you can't possibly know that. I got dressed in my closet this morning. No windows. The only one who saw me in there was my dog."

"Lucky Moscow."

"Pushing it, pal."

"Angel, everyone in the department knows about your Alaskan husky."

"Yeah, except I don't recall ever seeing you in the department. I also don't go around talking about my background. And my grandmother insists it's a Mayan connection." Wedging open a metal box, she sifted through the papers inside. "Other than Joe, how many spies do you have?"

"None, and that includes Joe. I pick up on details, I deduce. Sometimes I hit, just as often I miss. What are those papers you're rustling?"

"Receipts mostly. Some doodles." She grinned at one of the pages. "Hey, Foret really did like the Munsters. He drew Lily. Or—" she examined it more closely "—maybe it's Morticia."

"Who?"

"Buy a TV, okay?" Pushing the lid down, she continued along the counter. A tiny scraping sound reached her from the island. "Terrific." She glanced over it. "The rats probably are as big as were-wolves." She moved one of the food containers aside, then gave in, leaned her elbows on the counter and whispered, "It's ivory." She skimmed a finger across the buttons. "All lace, but not quite white."

"It's a tempting picture, Angel."

The tone of his voice brought a surprising rush of heat. But then could you tease a mystery man and not expect to pay the price? She really needed to let go of this particular fantasy.

Fanning her face, she continued her search.

A napkin smeared with soy sauce sat behind the metal box. Red markings showed through from the other side. Curious, she used gloved fingers to smooth the wrinkles.

And there it was.

"Oh, hell."

It was as far as she got. The scratching sound came again, followed by a low growl.

Movement exploded from behind the island. Angel saw bared teeth, gray arms and a pair of very large hands. A split second before she was tackled to the floor.

"ANGEL!"

Noah heard the growl as clearly as if it were a gunshot. When she didn't respond, he shouted her name again, then swore and grabbed his jacket. He kept his phone activated, snatched up his keys and held them in his mouth while he dragged on his boots.

The sounds of a struggle were unmistakable. Still swearing, he ran for the door.

No shots had been fired, but then Foret's killer didn't use a gun. Knives were silent. And equally fatal.

The attacker's breath whistled out. Noah knew Angel was good at hand-to-hand. She'd also be carrying a gun.

"Shoot him," he said through his teeth.

But still no shots reached him.

"Angel!" he tried again.

"Big, heavy jerk… Ouch! Damn."

Noah pounded through the alley exit and disarmed his truck. He almost tore the hinges off as he opened the door.

He was jamming the key into the ignition when he heard her vexed, "You're really pissing me off, pal. Face down, stay there and don't move. Don't twitch. Don't even breathe hard." Louder, she called, "Liz!" Then to the phone, "I'm okay, Noah. It's a vagrant."

"Street person," her assailant's voice sneered.

All the air left Noah's lungs. He let his forehead fall onto the steering wheel.

"You're breathing hard," Angel warned.

"What d'you expect, lady?" Her prisoner grunted. "You kicked me in the…"

"Angel?" Liz clattered in. "I heard a commotion… Ah. Who's he?"

"Street person. Noah, are you there?"

Drill the bastard, he thought, but breathed it out and managed a level, "Yeah, I'm here. What the hell's going on?" Not that he didn't know, but until his heart returned to his chest, he wanted her to do the talking.

"Just a trespasser," she answered lightly.

"Yeah, right, like you were invited in."

"A dirty trespasser," she continued, "who needs glasses desperately. I've been holding my ID in front of his nose for the past two minutes."

"Could be fake." The man snorted. "How do I know you're not running a grow op here? All I wanted to do was sleep where it's not wet."

"Move your hand another inch toward my gun and you'll be in a deeper sleep than you can imagine. Liz?"

"Call's in. Cops are coming."

Climbing out of his truck, Noah welcomed the sting of near-freezing rain on his face. "You sure you're not hurt?"

"Sore cheekbone," she told him. "He clipped me before I realized what was happening. Otherwise, I'm fine."

He pictured a bruise under one of her stunning hazel eyes, let the rain wash over his face while his system rebalanced.

"Noah?"

"Yeah."

"I've got the note."

"The what?" He had to drag his mind back, reorient.

"You told me to look for a note. Pretty sure I found it. It's written on a diner-style paper napkin. It's not the same as the napkins that came with the Chinese takeout, but it's definitely diner-like."

"Can you read it?"

"Clearly. Whoever did it printed the words in caps using one of those art supply stencils. You want cryptic? You got it. It says: SUFFERING IS THE BRIDGE TO UNDERSTANDING."

"MAYBE HE SEES HIMSELF as a martyr," she theorized later. "Pseudo and sick, but with the genuine belief that he's ridding the world of evil."

Liz waited for the server to deposit their lunch orders. "I went through the records last night,

Angel. Explain to me what's evil about a soccer mom with three kids who belonged to the PTA and baked cookies for her husband's geek squad computer repair coworkers."

"On the surface, nothing. But I checked the files, too. She lived in Danvers. Maybe she was a closet witch. Wicked as opposed to Wicca."

"You're grasping, partner."

"At really flimsy straws." Angel drummed her fingers. "The woman was killed eight years ago, yeah?"

"That's what Joe said Noah said."

Propping her chin in her hand, Angel nudged her bowl aside and let her mind wander. To an inappropriate place, she had to admit, but she was as human as the next person and female to boot.

"Liz, why will Noah let Joe see him and not me?"

Her partner swallowed a spoonful of Irish stew and groaned. "This is so good. If I knew, Angel, I'd tell you, I really would. For what it's worth, I haven't seen him either, or even spoken to him on the phone. No one I know has. Anyway." She used her index finger to scoop the hair from Angel's eyes. "You don't want to see him right now. That cheekbone of yours is bruising nicely."

Angel touched the mark, sighed, dropped her hand. "'Suffering is the bridge to understanding.' That's not cryptic, it's the inside of a fortune cookie."

"Written on a napkin, with a stencil."

"Noah says that's how the guy does it. He prints a piece of philosophical gibberish on a scrap of paper, or a napkin, or a candy bar wrapper and slips it to his victims. More often than not, and Foret's no exception, there's a partially eaten meal or half empty glass nearby. Which suggests a follow up form of contact at some point, instructing the victim to meet him."

"Or else…" Liz finished the threat.

Angel glanced over as her cell phone began to vibrate.

"Speak of the invisible devil." Liz dipped into her stew again. "Listen, I hate to beg favors of a man I've never met, but could you ask Mr. Graydon to stop beating my husband at chess? It's deflating to his ego, and we get enough of that from Graeme and his centerfold girlfriends."

"It's not Noah." Angel tried to stem the feeling of disappointment that made her want to ditch the call. But that was a childish response—and all the more disturbing for that reason. She picked up with a pleasant, "Hey, Brian. What's the news?"

"What's the noise?" her dour-sounding coworker countered.

The restaurant Angel and Liz had chosen played edgy flute music at mid-volume. The atmosphere was dusty Irish Goth, with the barest hint of an underlying maritime theme. Not that they could see the ocean, but they could certainly hear the storm blowing in from it as belts of wind battered the weathered outer walls.

"That," she replied, "is the sound of a glorious autumn rainfall in New England. Any prints on the napkin?"

"Only Foret's."

Angel massaged a spot on the back of her neck. "Brian, you were in Boston when the murders stopped five years ago. How many victims did the Penny Killer have?"

"How much wood could a wood chuck chuck…" He offered back a verbal shrug. "Seven that we know of, and I can still name them all."

She visualized him puffing up as he rattled off the list.

Brian Pinkney, better known as the Brain in Bureau circles, whizzed around the office on his electric wheelchair, getting in everyone's face and just as frequently on their nerves. He could walk—Angel had seen him do it—but after a car accident several years ago had left him with nerve damage to his spine, he preferred not to tax himself and usually rode instead. He was fifty-six years old, beefy, bald and seemed to sport a new tattoo every time he rolled up his sleeves. No one really liked him, but they couldn't deny he knew his stuff. Which was probably why he'd lobbied Bergman for the first crack at profiling the Penny Killer.

That he hadn't succeeded in his bid would make the lives of everyone in the office hell for a good long while, but as Angel saw it, life was all about facing challenges. Another one more or less wasn't likely to affect her day.

"Five of the victims came from Massachusetts," Brian continued now. "Two from Philadelphia. Three of the Massachusetts five lived in Boston. The others were from Danvers and New Bedford. Does that help you, or is your head still wobbling from that scrap you had this morning?"

"My head's fine." She rubbed her nape. "If the same guy's responsible for Foret's death, Bri, that pushes the Boston count to four, and both Danvers and New Bedford are an easy drive, so there's a better than average chance the killer lives here."

"Cheery thought, huh?"

"Yeah, if you're in L.A." She broke off a chunk of bread, but didn't eat it. "Some suspects would be good. So far, everyone we've connected to Foret is either alibied or out of reach. Case in point, his pal the Secretary."

"Guy's clean enough as politicians go."

Angel grinned. "Glad to know it." Then sighed. "You're profiling, aren't you?"

"My free time's my own." He sounded defensive and angry. "Bergman gave the job to Pruneface— Bill Skater. The guy has one speed: turtle."

"He's also Bergman's brother-in-law. Do the math."

"Did that creep at Foret's do something to your neck?" Liz asked.

"I—no." Angel frowned. "Why?" Then she realized she was rubbing the same spot again.

Still holding the phone, she peered around the side of the booth, but saw only tables, more booths and a roomful of people who were paying no attention to anything except their food.

"What?" Liz followed her gaze.

"Someone's watching us."

Her friend tugged her back by her hair. "Eat your stew, Angel. A full stomach'll make the feeling go away."

"I know how hungry feels, and it isn't hallucinogenic." She made another quick circuit. "Brian, does the killer stalk his victims?"

"Ask Skater."

She forced patience. "I'm asking you."

"Don't they all?"

"Okay, well that doesn't make me feel any better, actually. Liz, we need to lose the Goth cafés for a while."

"Food's good at this one." Liz spooned up more stew. "Not that you'd know, since all you've done is play with your bread."

"Oh, hell." Angel's eyes fixed on the door. "Paul Reuben just slithered in. And he's wearing his media hat."

"There's the last bite done, thank you, God." Liz wiped her mouth and fingers. "How does he always know?"

"Afternoon, ladies." At Liz's exasperated look,

he pressed an exaggerated hand to his chest. "What am I supposed to say? Afternoon, Feds?"

Angel smiled. "'I just stopped in to say good-bye' works."

"Thanks, I'd love to join you." He scraped a chair across the floor and straddled it.

"You know, Paul, it's just possible we're busy here." Angel waved her cell phone. "You want a story, talk to Bergman's assistant. That's why he's there."

Paul Reuben's flinty eyes gleamed. "Is Noah Graydon helping you with your busy work?"

"Go away." She enunciated the words, then smacked at his hand. "Touch my lunch, and I'll cite you for something really unpleasant."

When her skin continued to prickle, she glanced around again. An old man in a hat with earflaps stared back at her. So did a much younger one with a heavily pierced face.

"Do me a favor, Paul, take a stroll and check out the booths."

"For what?"

"Perverts, peeping Toms." She summoned a sweet smile. "Murderers."

"Like the one who offed Lionel Foret early Sunday morning behind a dockside processing plant?"

"There you go. If you know that much, you're as up to date as we are. Bye."

"Cut the guy some slack, Angel," Brian suggested on the phone. "He might know something."

"He might also be fishing."

"What's the deal with Graydon?" the reporter persisted. "Is he in or out? Give me that much at least."

Angel rested her chin on her fist, let her smile ride. "How did you hear about Foret, Paul?"

"I got a tip."

"Where and from whom?"

"None of your business—on both counts."

"Okay then, we're done. Drive carefully."

He appealed to Liz. "Your husband's tight with Graydon, right?"

Elbows on the table, Liz pushed on her temples. "You know, I didn't have a headache when I came in."

Paul started slurping hot coffee—and Angel found her own fingers straying under her hair again.

Determined to shake the sensation, she returned her attention to Brian. "Do I know yet why you called?"

"Not unless you're a mind reader. I've been instructed to tell you that Bergman's staying over in Washington. He tried your cell, but the line was tied up. Would that have been before or after your run-in with a sleeping vagrant?"

"Street person, and he topped your two-thirty by a good ten pounds."

"Using?"

"Definitely."

"You know, I was once as quick as you are, and as elusive as Noah Graydon when I chose to be."

"You sound bitter, Bri." Sliding to the end of the booth, she made another casual sweep of the restaurant. "Get some physio, get in shape and presto, you're back in the field."

"On restricted duty. No thanks, kid. Don't forget to check in with Bergman's lackey before you go off shift. And have fun detaching your investigative burr."

Angel ended the call with a distracted press of the button. Her eyes traveled from table to table. "Got to be coming from a booth. I can see everyone else."

Reuben waved a hand in front of her face. "Why the space flight, Angel?"

Looking back, she noted that his mustache, blonde and perpetually droopy, was saturated with coffee. "Trust me, Paul, there are times when outer space is preferable to planet Earth."

He snagged her wrist as someone in black brushed past. "If you won't talk about Graydon, explain the pennies on Foret's eyelids."

Liz breathed out. "Don't you have…?" Then she stopped, met Angel's eyes, and bent forward over the table. "Well, well, Mr. Reuben."

At a similar look from Angel, the reporter released her. "Okay, why have you two turned cat all of a sudden?"

But he knew. Angel could tell by the dull red

flush creeping up his neck that he understood exactly what he'd done.

Smiling, she crooked a leg up and turned companionably toward him. "Playing dumb isn't your strong suit, PR. Guess what? There was no mention of any pennies in our official statement. Only a handful of people saw the body, and those who did wouldn't have talked. So—" Brows arched, she cocked her head to observe. "How is it you managed to find out about them?"

THE DAY AFTER A DEATH always felt long—going through the motions, controlling jitters, concentrating. Slipping up was too damned easy, in big ways and in small.

But things had to be put right, and no one else appeared to want the job.

Someone would have to take it on, though, because the end was approaching. Fast. The Thanksgiving season seemed an appropriate time for the finale. Give thanks to the only person who understood.

Extra caution would be needed to pull this last one off. Extra caution and nerves of steel.

An image swam up, solidified. No second thoughts. No regrets. It must and would be done.

Target date: Third week of November.

Target victim: Angel Carter.

Chapter Four

No one Angel knew, except maybe her uncle who
ran whale-watching charters out of Juneau, could
talk for hours and in the end say nothing. No one,
except a reporter like Paul Reuben.

"I know how to get into people's heads,
Moscow." She deposited her keys on a tray inside
her front door. "I know how to get into a rat's head
even better, and I got nowhere with that guy. I want
a hot bath, anything I don't have to cook and a big
glass of Chardonnay." She knelt to ruffle the
husky's ears. "So how was your day?"

Pawing the shoulder of her red leather jacket, he
nosed her toward the phone.

"Someone called?"

He barked.

"Someone you hear on my voice mail, but never
see? A man whose face I try to paint, but who
keeps coming out looking like Lamont Cranston's
alter ego?"

Shedding her jacket and bag, she headed for the

bathroom. After washing her hands and splashing cold water on her face, she felt better, not totally alert, but functional. She changed into a pair of drawstring pants and a T, pulled her hair into a high ponytail, left her feet bare and went into the kitchen.

Hot cocoa, she thought with a roll of her head to loosen the tight muscles. "And one doggie treat," she told the expectant husky. She held up a single finger. "One."

As she passed the phone, she hit the retrieve button on her voice mail. At maximum volume, the messages came through clearly.

"Hi, Angel, it's Pete Peloni, from Peloni's Place. You left your sunglasses on the table last time you were here. Also, I'm trying out a new mushroom-veggie pizza with hot pepper sauce. I'm working most of tonight and all day tomorrow. I'll drop off a sample on my way home. Catch you later."

Angel regarded the package of instant cocoa in her hand and laughed as she shook it down. "You're not likely to convert me, Pete, but my mother would appreciate the effort."

Brian Pinkney followed. "It's after seven, Monday night, Angel. Thought you'd be home by now. I wouldn't do this for anyone except you and Liz, so consider yourself privileged, but I ran the comps on all the Penny Killer murders. Highlighted the similarities, and also took care of the B-side—the irregularities. Basically, I did some major decluttering for you. It's more than Prune-face Skater would have done. Info's waiting in a file labeled Angel's PKMs. I have to say, this one's a stumper. Hope you like coffee and caffeine pills, sweetheart. You're gonna need 'em."

Next up, Graeme Thomas wanted her to fly to Atlantic City with him for a convention the following weekend. "They have wedding chapels there, too," he remarked with a wink in his voice that made her chuckle as she poured boiling water into a big "I Love Bullwinkle's Cousins" mug.

Twenty minutes later, he called again. "Sorry, babe. Change of plans. Looks like I'll be doing double duty at the Victim Support Center this weekend. Would you believe that one of the families I've been counseling has lost three of their kids to murder and drunk drivers in less than five years? Some people have absolutely no luck. How's the Boardwalk between Christmas and New Year's sound to you…?"

Wandering into the solarium she used as a painting studio, Angel hoisted herself onto a high stool, blew into the steaming mug and studied her latest canvas. The face she'd attempted to paint had no definition, only blurred and shadowed features. Still, something of the man came through for her.

"Probably because I know it's you," she reflected, and touched his mouth with an exploratory fingertip.

Her doctor's office called next—she'd missed

an appointment—and then Bergman's pushy assistant, three times. Pete came back, on adding a soy cheese and green vegetable pizza to the revised menu, and finally, finally, the one she'd been hoping for. Noah Graydon.

Unfortunately, all he said was, "Read your e-mails, Angel."

She sighed at the painting. "You know I prefer verbal communication, Noah. I can't hear you in an e-mail."

Licking whipped cream from the rim of her mug, she vacated her stool and headed for the computer.

The first e-mail was from Joe and directed her to a restricted FBI site, where she viewed Lionel Foret's autopsy results.

The forensic team had discovered only microscopic fibers and Foret's own skin cells under his fingernails. There'd been one bird feather and several strands of his own hair on his coat. Joe placed the time of death between midnight and 12:30 a.m. He said he'd have put it closer to twelve, except Foret had been wearing thermal underwear, so he'd needed to allow for a cocoon effect.

"Let me know who won the pool," Joe typed. "Also, my wife told me to tell you that you must come for Thanksgiving dinner. Bring your mom and her trucker if they're in town. Oh, and her Harley—that's for me. FYI, Jaynie loves her new pink shoes. She told me to thank Auntie Angel again.

"Not wanting to mix business with pleasure, but I'm sorry for the delay on the Foret case. One of my techs mislaid the results. We found them in the file of a Balinese man who died three days ago from ptomaine poisoning. Don't be a stranger…"

"As if I could." Hitting a key, she moved on to Noah's message. Her cell phone, doing a sudden dance across the desk, interrupted her.

"Tell me you didn't just get home."

Noah's sexy drawl brought a swell of regret to Angel's throat.

"Ten minutes ago." Blanking the monitor, she crossed to the window seat, tucked herself into the lotus position and sipped. "Multiple messages, minimum lights. I made hot cocoa, but I probably should have made up an ice pack instead." She probed her bruised cheek. "Gonna need major makeup tomorrow."

"I don't like that picture, Angel. How bruised are we talking?"

"It's not a black eye, and the guy only got me because I tripped over a piece of pipe. Totally clumsy."

"Somehow I doubt that."

"Did you hear? Bergman's got Prune—uh, Bill Skater working the profile for the Penny Killer. Brian Pinkney's really pissed off."

"How can you tell?"

She laughed, considered briefly as she surveyed the glittering city skyline visible above the park side trees, then said, "Noah, have I ever told you that I play chess?"

"Pretty sure that's a no."

"Well, I do. Long Alaska nights, wicked blizzards, gen power running low, so no movies, no *Dancing with the Stars*..."

Noah breathed out whatever he was feeling. Annoyance, frustration, resignation.

The sound sent a shimmer of guilt through her system. "Look, I'm tired, okay, and a little cranky. I wasn't..."

"You don't want to meet me, Angel."

Humor trickled in. "An amazing profiler, and he reads minds, too. Not accurately, but what can you expect over a phone line? Come on, Noah, even Spock's Vulcan mind meld required a certain amount of physical contact. And if you ask me who Spock is, I'll be convinced you live in space instead of him."

"Call it a shadow world."

"You're not going to answer me, are you?"

"The Internet has game partners..."

"Go there," she warned, "and I'm hanging up. I also give up. Temporarily." Turning slightly, she zeroed in on the area where she thought he lived. "Why the call?"

"Because you're still on the clock at 10:00 p.m."

"And you're not?"

"I do my best work at night."

Not chess, but a game of strategy nonetheless. His words flowed through her like warm brandy, seducing her far more than they probably should. Angel's stomach muscles quivered and her skin felt unnaturally hot. But seduction was a thing she could match in her sleep.

Running a finger over her cell, she rested her back on the wall and let a note of teasing humor invade her voice. "It might come as a surprise to you, Noah, but night's one of my best times, too. Or so I've been told."

His hesitation spoke volumes. So did his tone when he said, "Below the belt, Angel, in more ways than one."

Now that *was* the point. But did hearing it change anything?

Moscow barked. Twisting the mouthpiece upward, she asked him, "What is it?" She told Noah, "Dog's excited.,"

The husky ran to the door, paused at the jamb. A second later, she heard a knock.

"That'll be Pete." Uncrossing her legs, she took another sip of cocoa, then stretched like a cat. "He says I'm a bad eater. Keeps trying to push tofu and veggie pizza on me."

"Pete?"

Was there a frown attached to the question? Might be worth playing—to a point.

"Pete Peloni. He's a guy I know. Tall. Very attractive. Really nice. He runs Peloni's Place in Little Italy. It's a sort of Italian restaurant with an upscale vibe, about ten blocks from the processing plant where Foret was killed. No segue intended. Liz and I go there sometimes for lunch. I guess she likes tofu... Yes, I'm coming, Moscow." But she hesitated halfway to the door. "Why *did* you call, Noah?"

"I found a shoe site."

"Excuse me?"

"Women's shoes, thousands of them. It's a French site. Designer boots and shoes at knock-off prices. Proof that one or two of my ancestors did in fact come from Europe."

Delight mingled with astonishment. Delight won, hands down.

"I'll go there tonight," she promised, "and let you know tomorrow how big a hit my credit card takes." With a motion to silence Moscow, she added a soft, "Thanks, Noah," and ended the call. "Yes, I'm here," she told the excited husky "Why the fuss?" Placing her palm on the frame, she looked through the viewer.

The corridor was empty.

"Took too long, huh? Well, it couldn't have been Pete. He'd have left a bag of goodies big enough to feed everyone in the building."

Which was only three other tenants, since the "building," once a huge post-Revolution mansion, had been converted into four large condos. But

Pete believed in stocked fridges as deeply as he believed in healthy eating.

Angel started to turn away. Then she frowned and did a double take through the viewer.

No box sat on the polished hallway floor—but something else did. After a quick second sweep, she snicked the bolt and opened the door.

It could have been a discarded grocery list lying there, but Angel's instincts suggested otherwise. With Moscow sniffing the air, she used the back of her index finger to flick the paper over.

And seeing the words printed there, breathed a heartfelt, "Damn."

NOAH HEARD THE WHIR of an approaching motor, followed by wheels rolling over damp pavement. From his crouch, and without looking back, he acknowledged the new arrival.

"Been a while, old friend."

"Oh, just a few years. Like say—five?"

The belligerent thrust said it all. Noah half smiled at the ground. "Let me guess, you're angry with Bergman."

"Wouldn't you be? He's letting Pruneface Skater do the profile on this guy. So far all I've heard is that the killer's a male—wow, that took a brain the size of Everest to figure—right-handed and he gets his victims from behind. A chimp could have told us that much, and a hell of a lot quicker than Pruneface did."

"What do you want, Brian?"

The wheels ground closer. "Same as you. To nail the bastard who turned you into a ghost and me into a cripple."

Noah reviewed the outline of Foret's body that he'd drawn from memory. "You crippled yourself, and I withdrew by choice. We can't blame a madman for everything."

"No, we can't do that. Some of the blame has to fall on other shoulders."

And here it came, Noah thought.

The wheelchair gave a whiny rev. "The kid was green, Noah. You were supposed to be training him. That was the deal. Instead, you let him meet a murderer alone, with no backup and no idea what he was getting into."

Noah stood slowly, felt the metal basket push into the side of his long coat. "What is it you want? Blood from a stone? Not gonna happen. Blood from another victim? Already done. You knew the killer wasn't dead, and so did I."

"That fire…"

"Only destroyed the warehouse and its contents."

"The investigating agents said the flames were hot enough to incinerate bone."

"But they didn't." Noah turned his head halfway. "Because there were no bones to burn, and when the fire was out, only another victim in the morgue. You drove too fast, I didn't move fast enough, and it didn't end that night."

"And all of it, every last frigging scrap, was your fault, you bast…"

"Don't." Noah switched his gaze to the water. "You want to be bitter, go ahead. You want to wallow, be my guest. But don't roll up to me on the spot where another victim lost his life and try to blame me for everything that went wrong that night. For what's always been wrong in your life."

Red-faced, Brian circled until they faced each other. "And your life's just peachy, is it? Exactly the way you want it to be? Tell me you're not bitter, that you're not wallowing, that you don't blame yourself for what happened. Tell me, and we'll both have a good laugh."

His voice trembled but whether from fury or sorrow, Noah couldn't say. In any case, he softened his attitude and his expression. "It shouldn't have gone the way it did. I should have known the kid would go off half-cocked with a bellyful of something to prove. Not sure if the proving was for your benefit or mine, but it doesn't matter. He was green. I wasn't. I should have seen it coming."

Brian's knuckles whitened on the steering handles. "Is that supposed to make me feel better— you admitting you were wrong?"

A faint smile touched Noah's mouth. In the pocket of his coat his cell phone began to vibrate. "Not particularly. Just thought it should be said. The past's done, Brian. Your feelings are your own. But I want this guy—for a lot of reasons."

"And because you can't be on the case, you're prepared to use Angel to get him. No matter what the cost."

Noah simply stared until Brian spun with a jerk. Slapping the motorized vehicle in gear, he zoomed through the shadows and into the access way.

But not before Noah glimpsed the glitter of contempt in his eyes—and the twist of hatred he didn't bother to hide on his lips.

"NOT GOING TO OVERREACT," Angel promised herself. "I've been threatened before and will again. This isn't new." With the phone to her ear, she paced the perimeter of her living room floor. "Pick up, Graydon. We were talking less than twenty minutes ago."

"Didn't like the shoes, huh?" he said at last.

Stopping at the window, she let her eyes flit to the park across the street. "Much as I love the sexy drawl, I got a note."

That killed it. "When?" he demanded.

No what, only when, in a whip-sharp tone that had nothing to do with sexy. "Maybe twenty minutes ago. I followed procedure, checked out the stairwells and doors, front and back. Whoever delivered it was gone. My neighbors who are home didn't see a thing. There are no foot or tire prints." She dragged the elastic band from her hair, blew out a breath. "How does this guy choose his victims, Noah? I have no connection to Foret. I'm not a soccer mom with three kids, a biotech who analyzes ocean fungus, or the CEO of a national supermarket chain. Yes, there was an FBI agent on the list of victims, along with a cop and another lawyer, but we're talking years of separation and no link between them that anyone could find, including you, who'd have dug up whatever was diggable. So all that leaves is the fact that I'm working this case." A sudden thought brought her head around with a snap. "Oh, my God, Liz!"

"Calm down, Angel."

She raked the hair from her face, held it there. Breathed. And again. "I am calm. I am," she repeated. "Perfectly. That babble was just me sorting through the confusion." Crossing to the land phone, she punched her partner's number.

"Is Liz at home?"

"No idea. I'm calling her cell—which, of course, she's not answering… Liz, it's Angel. I need you to call me back. It's urgent…" She swung around. "Noah, are we talking about a multiple-target killer here? You know, threaten a new victim before he's disposed of another?"

His lack of response wasn't encouraging. She entered her partner's home number, then tried Joe on his cell, leaving urgent messages on both.

"Moscow, come away from the window." She caught his collar with two fingers. "Why me, Noah? Because of the case or not?"

"Angel…"

"I know, I know." She tugged harder. "You don't know." Frustration battled fear. And thankfully beat it back. "What's that sound?"

"My truck. Stay inside. Doors and windows locked, lights off. I'll handle the follow-up."

"I promise you, the guy's gone. I even went through my upstairs neighbor's condo. I'm watering her plants while she's away for the holidays. There was no one."

"Humor me, okay?"

She heard a squeal of tires. "Well, yeah—if you get here. The door's bolted, and Moscow may be young, but he's trained. I have two guns, I was top ten in hand-to-hand, and I've got adrenaline to spare at this point."

"Use it to think. Just make sure you do it inside your place."

"I'm not…"

"Promise me, Angel."

The words wanted to stick. However… "Okay, I promise. On one condition."

"And that is?"

Another squeal had her wincing. "Make it two. First, that you slow down, and second, that you don't tell Bergman about this."

"No."

Frustration bled into exasperation. "Why not? And don't be obtuse. Foret's not the only person with connections in the capitol. My uncle's a congressman."

"Retired and living in Juneau."

"I said don't be obtuse."

"This isn't a game, Angel."

"I'm not playing one. This is my life and my case. If Bergman pulls me off, I'll simply investigate on my own time, without partner or backup."

"The note you got tonight is evidence. You'd have to withhold it. Federal offense, Agent Carter."

"I'll have it analyzed for prints and all the usual etceteras. Fully aware here, Graydon, whatever you might think."

A final squeal of brakes told her he'd arrived. She couldn't resist, she returned to the window and stared at the street below.

It had to be Noah who climbed from the large, black truck. His coat was long and, she suspected, also black. In fact, everything about him appeared black, even his hair, which she thought might skim his shoulders. She couldn't tell because he was wearing a hat with a broad brim and, since it was still raining, had his collar turned up.

He was definitely tall. Over six feet, with a long stride and, she imagined, a lean build.

Unfortunately, no features were visible, and she only had a glimpse to go on as the shadows of the old house swallowed him up within seconds of his arrival.

Moscow wedged himself between her and the ledge and pushed on her legs.

"Okay." She gave his side an appreciative pat. "Backing away."

But she glanced toward the solarium. It felt downright spooky that she would have painted Noah almost exactly as she'd seen him tonight. A shadow within a shadow.

"I'm in."

"What? Oh." She'd forgotten about the active phone connection. A frown, then, "In the building?"

"I've already gone through the lobby."

Not going to ask, she decided. "Noah?"

"Stay where you are," he repeated.

"Yes, I got that part. I thought you'd like to know what the note said."

"I was getting to it." But he sounded distracted which probably meant he was searching again. "Go ahead, I'm listening."

She unhooked and lowered the blind, didn't need to see the words to recall them. "It said: THE CIRCLE OF UNDERSTANDING WILL BE COMPLETE AT LAST. He stenciled it on a scrap of yellow newsprint, the kind you use for notes in college." She heard boots on the stair treads and added, "I went through the basement, too."

"Did I mention the part about humoring me?"

"Did I mention the part about not telling Bergman?"

"Can't hear you, Angel. Bad reception."

"That's not very original." When he didn't respond, she sighed, "Come on, Noah."

Only silence reached her.

She debated for a moment, then shrugged and

dropped the phone in the pocket of her pants. "In that case, ditto." Pulling on her coat and boots, she picked up her gun, motioned to Moscow and slipped into the hall's period lighting, glowing and romantic, perfect for a nineteenth-century mansion.

But the shadows that might have been deemed intimate in their day created a much less appealing atmosphere right now. Angel angled her gun toward the coffered ceiling as she started down the stairs.

Because the first-floor neighbors were abnormally nosy, she knew all the creaks and how to avoid them. Moscow padded ahead of her. Angel retrieved her cell and brought it to her ear.

"Noah, are you there?"

No answer.

Had the communication really broken up? Builders had added a layer of concrete between the first floor and cellar. It was possible, she supposed, if a little too convenient.

"Noah?"

Still no response.

"Don't think I'm liking this, Moscow. Be very quiet."

The dog's ears twitched, but he obeyed.

The shadows deepened on the first floor, because, of course, no one had bothered to replace the burned out light near the basement door.

"Noah?" She called his name, first into her cell and again down the narrow cellar stairwell.

The single shaft of light trickling upward didn't quite reach the top. Use the main switch, or take a chance and creep down in the semidarkness? Either way, she could wind up shot.

She opted to creep, on the off chance that the killer was still lurking. Noah would be too well trained to shoot first and ask questions later. She hoped.

"Behind me, Moscow."

She made one last attempt to raise Noah on her cell. When he didn't answer, she disconnected. Liz might be trying to call her, although she hadn't noticed a vibration from her caller alert. Maybe Joe had taken his wife out for a late dinner.

She counted down fourteen steps, used her free hand for balance on the wall and kept her gun up.

Moscow gave a prolonged growl—not a promising sign.

"Stay back," she ordered, then peered into the gloom. "Noah?"

Eyes moving, she sketched the layout. Bike room dead ahead, furnace room to the left, storage right. The cellar smelled of old earth, old bricks and centuries' old wood. But strangely, the faint scent of apples superceded all those things in Angel's mind, and gave the place a sense of nostalgia that took her back to her grandmother's Iowa root cellar.

She'd played hidden ghost there with her cousins several times as a child—until nasty cousin Billy had grabbed her ankle from under the stairs and almost given her a coronary.

Moscow growled again. Angel accepted the shiver that rippled along her spine. Had the darkness shifted?

The growl became a barely muffled bark. The dog's muscles bunched against her thigh. Setting a hand on his head, she stilled him.

She felt it, too. Something about the air had altered. She made a cautious half circle, saw nothing. But there was a sound. A movement. A faint swish of motion that bordered on invisible.

Was it the killer down here, or Noah? Or neither? She'd found a junkie outside the bike room once, curled up and virtually comatose. She still had no idea how he'd gotten in.

The third time Moscow barked, there was nothing muffled about it. His ears went flat back, and he showed his teeth.

Angel spun, but she was too slow. She encountered only a tower of black. The tower was mobile, and it blocked both escape and advance. Before she could bring her gun down, a pair of hands seized her wrist and swung her around.

"Don't move," her captor said into her ear. He shifted so the fingers of his right hand formed a V around the upper part of her throat. "Very good," he congratulated when she froze. "Now, call off your dog, and lower your gun to the ground."

Chapter Five

Angel's sharply drawn breath hissed out. "One more person grabs me in a cellar, and I'm going to sink my teeth into his arm. Friend, Moscow," she said, then twitched her shoulders and set her heel on the booted toe behind her. "I should and still might spike you, Graydon. That wasn't funny."

"It wasn't meant to be."

He held her against him. Tightly. Lean, her mind acknowledged, and very well muscled, like a thoroughbred stallion.

Her mouth curved into a reluctant smile at the comparison. She was more rattled than she'd thought.

"You can let go, Noah. I couldn't see you in this light if I wanted to."

"I told you to stay inside."

Ignoring her subtle struggles, he kept his mouth next to her ear. His breath stirred her hair. Another shiver, this one rooted in something more disturbing than fear, tripped through her.

"Lots of people tell me lots of things in a day. I don't do most of them." When he still didn't release her, she used her proximity to try and judge his height. "Six-two?" she guessed.

"Six-three, and if I was the killer, you'd be dead."

"Don't count on it. You do realize, the more you play the Invisible Man, the more curious people will become. No pictures on file, no one in the office who can or will talk about you. Even Brian clams up when your name's mentioned, and I know he was in Boston when the first group of murders went down."

"He was, I wasn't. Not posted here anyway. I came and went. I hung around to work the investigation as a favor to your boss, but I've never been big on office appearances."

"Which makes you as mysterious as the note I got tonight. Curiosity level goes off the scale."

She caught the slight smile in his voice when he asked, "What's Skater given you so far?"

"What you'd expect. Male, strong, fit. Attacks his victims from the rear. Cuts left to right, which is why it's always the left carotid that gets slashed."

"Other side's been slashed as well."

"After the fact, though, right?"

"It's a secondary slice," Noah agreed. "Inflicted after death or very close to."

"Which means?"

"Either a poor attempt at a cover-up or a deliberate taunt."

"Which do you think?"

"Leaning toward the taunt."

"But obviously not a hundred percent. Why?"

"Because this guy's more clever than cocky. He has an ego, but there's a deeper purpose. He's saying something in his notes. The words 'bridge', 'understand' and 'circle' come up repeatedly."

"What about the word 'complete'?"

"Never used it before."

"Which is?"

"Not good."

She sighed. "I don't know about you, Graydon, but I've had better nights. Uh, could you move your hand? I'm having trouble concentrating, and this stuff's important."

The fingers on her throat slid downward to settle lightly on her upper arm.

Moscow barked and wagged his tail. Considering what he'd just told her, Angel couldn't believe she wanted to laugh. Or maybe she could. "It isn't fair, you know. Joe and my dog get to see you, but I don't. You're not shy, so why the fixation with shadows?

"You haven't heard the rumors?"

"I don't listen to gossip, or more accurately in your case, speculation."

"That's not an answer."

She shuddered lightly as his lips brushed her cheek. This wasn't going quite the way she'd hoped. Or maybe it was more that the direction was off.

"Yes, I've heard the rumors." She made a point of relaxing into him. "I've also painted you forty or fifty times. All I end up with is a silhouette." Her eyes strayed to the fingers on her arms. Long, strong, very much as she imagined him to be. But still with limited definition.

"Don't, Angel."

She masked a swell of desire with an amused, "Do you really expect me to understand that?"

"You're trying to distract me with your body."

Both desire and amusement deepened. "Is it working?"

"It would work on a robot."

She moved her hips just enough to tease. Or torment. Depended on his control, her effect and their chemistry. From Angel's perspective, the last thing felt highly combustible. But whether they'd explode in the good or bad way remained to be seen.

What she wanted to do was turn and slide her arms around his neck. To see him, yes, but more than that, to pull his mouth onto hers and taste him, to know, really know, if the feelings racing around inside her were real or merely a fantasy she'd created from the darkness and his voice.

"Stop it, Angel."

There was no sting in his tone, only a murmur of sound that made her want to push it and him that much farther.

He smelled like rain. Fresh, clean and oddly

sensual. But she'd had dreams about Noah Graydon, and sensual was only a starting point in most of them.

His lips grazed her cheek. "You need to stop this. Now."

She rested her head against his neck. "You're the one doing the holding, Noah, not me."

It was probably the wrong thing to say, certainly the wrong thing to do. Her lungs felt hot inside. Her skin sizzled. And she couldn't begin to interpret the sensations that spun like crazed dervishes through her stomach.

He let his lips skim across her cheek one last time, before dropping his hands and stepping back.

"This is why I don't come near you," he said simply.

Was that self-derision in his voice? She couldn't read him, and because of that, didn't turn. "Nothing you say will make me believe you're a monster. Or a pariah. Or whatever it is you imagine yourself to be. I'll push a little because that's my nature, but I won't trick you, and I won't look if you don't want me to."

He remained close enough that she could feel his breath in her hair. "You have a considerate nature, Angel."

"Depends on my mood how far considerate goes. My father's wife describes me a little differently."

She wanted to lean into him again, but didn't

move. Didn't breathe or even think, until Moscow gave a small bark and the heat inside her began to abate.

She knew he was gone. Silently—though how he'd pulled that off with boots and wooden stairs, she had no idea. But there was only air behind her now. Air and shadow and the memory of him, drifting like a silvery mist through her head.

"That was very weird, Moscow." She ran a palm over the wood railing, tapped it. "I can't believe I didn't look." With a final exasperated tap, she followed the dog up the stairs. "No, I'm into torment and frustration, because God knows I don't have enough of either thing in my life right now."

Moscow trotted to the front door while Angel switched off the cellar light and secured the lock. She heard Mrs. Clausen talking to someone, smelled cannoli and half smiled at her neighbor's customary complaints to the delivery person.

Seesawing her head, she called to Moscow, turned the corner for the first floor stairwell…

And slammed face first into a very large, very solid human chest.

NOAH DIDN'T LEAVE right away. It was the first time he'd been to Angel's home and he was curious to know more about it. For security reasons, he told himself, then gave a humorless chuckle and shoved the lie away.

She'd rented in the South End when she'd first

come to Boston, but she'd bought and settled in the North. He doubted if she knew he lived only five blocks away, or that he'd eaten at Pete Peloni's more times than he could count.

And speaking of Pete Peloni...

Noah recognized the restaurant owner's Ford Bronco by its dented front fender and duct-taped headlight. Angel had said Pete planned to bring her dinner tonight. Obviously, he'd come through; however, since he was climbing into and not out of his truck, she obviously hadn't asked him to stay.

None of his business one way or the other, Noah reminded himself, but he propped a shoulder on the side wall and watched Pete shake rain from the backward baseball cap he wore as a matter of habit.

A movement in the passenger seat caught Noah's eye. Pete's door hadn't completely closed. The interior light remained on, rendering the second occupant clearly visible.

Interesting. His gaze flicked to the building behind him. Angel's condo was on the second floor, front. Pete had come out the back door. Someone else had just gone in the main entrance.

And all of this activity less than an hour after Angel had received a note from a killer.

Connected or not? It seemed unlikely, but if nothing else, it went to prove that few people got away clean. Everyone had their burdens, their demons, their guilt. Their secrets.

What most of them didn't have was a killer after them.

Noah waited until Pete's door closed and his truck rolled away from the curb. Then he flipped up the collar of his coat, and melted into the darkness.

"I'M REALLY SORRY about Monday night, Angel." It was the first thing Joe said when she pushed through the path lab door late Thursday afternoon. "Like I told you, I got home late and couldn't find Liz anywhere, so I figured she must be with you. Noah was out, and no one knows where Graeme goes when he's not in surgery. I haven't connected with him since before you were spirited off to Washington. The pizza we had was interesting, though. Do gifts like that appear on your doorstep often?"

"Lots of things appear on my doorstep." Angel spotted a sheet-draped body and hovered near the wall. "Is that the guy I'm supposed to look at?"

"Sorry to say, it is. If you ask me, there's a bad copycat at work. But the cops won't take a stand yet, and you know Bergman."

"Mmm. Have an agent verify while I sip champagne with a roomful of political bigwigs." Angel drew her hands from the pockets of her coat, wiggled her fingers. "First he drags me to DC to placate Foret's old college buddy in person, then he gets word from assistant Snively and suddenly

I'm on a northbound plane. Why do I always get stuck with morgue detail?"

"Because you hate doing paperwork, and Liz excels in that area. Did she tell you about her great-aunt Trudy?"

"Aunt who?" Reluctantly, Angel tied her hair back.

"The person she went to see Monday night."

"I just got back to Boston, Joe. We haven't talked about Monday night yet." Not from Liz's perspective, at any rate.

"The old dear had an oven fire. Reduced two Cornish hens to black ash. She fell asleep in the middle of a cooking show."

"Sounds like my kind of woman." Angel knew Joe was watching her. She also knew why. The conversation was purely for show.

She snapped on a pair of latex gloves while mentally preparing herself to observe another pasty gray corpse. "You want to know why I didn't tell you about Noah and me in the cellar, right?"

His sandy brows went up. "Five minutes couldn't have passed since you'd been with him, yet you never even mentioned his name, let alone that you'd seen him."

"I didn't see him," she said. "That's the problem."

"Why was he there?"

"He thought I was in danger."

"Why did he think that? And why the urgent calls to me and Liz?"

"Because I thought she might be in danger. Look, it wasn't what either of us thought, okay? I'm sorry you've had to live with this for three days, but it was nothing. Just let it go."

He studied her through slightly fogged lenses. "You're withholding, Angel. Liz, too. I can see the strain in her eyes. The killer's after you, isn't he?"

How much should she confide, Angel wondered. "It's possible," she allowed. "We're not sure. Anyway, you have to figure the guy's not going to appreciate having the FBI on his tail. Sometimes perps turn and attack. It isn't like we haven't dealt with it before." She drew an air line over the lumpy sheet. "This guy was killed close to dawn this morning, right? Why do you think it's a copycat?"

"There were no pennies on his eyelids, or so I was told, only a handful of loose change scattered on the ground at his feet. His wallet was missing. So were any other valuables he might have been carrying. And from a medical standpoint, on top of being slashed, he was also stabbed through he heart. Not much blood involved, so my guess is he was dead by the time the knife went in. Still, it's inconsistent and therefore noteworthy."

"Does he have a name?"

"John Doe."

"Oh, good. Always love those. Anything else before we get to the fun part?"

"Well, yeah, one thing."

"You're squirming, Joe. I don't like that."

"You remember I said there were no pennies on his eyelids?"

Angel regarded the pale blue sheet, wished she could make what was under it disappear. "I'm not going to feel well when I leave here, am I?"

The odd tilt of his lips provided little encouragement. "Don't think so. I'm not clear on the whole penny scenario, but in this case, I can tell you that placing them on the victim's lids would have been impossible. To do that," Joe drew the sheet back, "he would need to have had eyes."

BY SIX O'CLOCK, Angel could actually think about food in an abstract sense. But she wasn't quite ready to eat it.

"Chicken cannelloni with red and green lumpy things." A foil container landed on her desk, courtesy of Brian, who'd been gruff and irritable all day. "Some lumberjack named Pete dropped it off for you downstairs."

Liz passed by with a stack of computer disks in her hand. "I don't think she's ready for red and green things, Brian. Maybe you'd like to take it home for dinner."

"Because I couldn't possibly have a date, could I, Ms. Thomas?"

Angel ignored his hostile tone, fingered the shiny container. "Any word on our John Doe yet?"

He waved a hand. "Spec is he's a mid-level dealer, possibly Boston-based. Bergman wants you and Liz to work with the cops, but concentrate on Foret's death. It's rumored there's a group of South American baddies currently working the Eastern seaboard who've been known to gouge out eyeballs when they think someone's crossed them. My opinion? Go with Doc Thomas, and label it a copycat."

"Makes two of you on board with that theory. What does Prune—ah, Skater think?"

"What am I, his messenger?"

"Just trying to save a little time here, Bri. Skater's office is three flights down, and he ignores phone calls."

"Probably can't find his phone for the mess on his desk. He's fence walking, says some aspects of the guy's death fit, others don't. Big news, huh?" His beefy shoulders hunched. "Stick with your own source, Angel. You're better off."

The advice appeared to leave a bad taste in his mouth, although why he disliked Noah so much eluded her. The answer was buried in the Restricted Access file that only Bergman and a select few others were permitted to see, she assumed.

"Something else?" she asked when he didn't shoot off.

He bared his teeth. "What is Graydon's read anyway?"

Angel smiled. "Now how would I know that?" Then she relented. "I haven't talked to Noah since I got back from DC. On the case or off, I'm sure he'll have an opinion. I'll let you know what it is when I hear it." She could probably handle coffee, she decided. Strong and black with lots of sugar. Pushing back, she stood. "Thanks for the info, Brian. The cannelloni's yours if you want it."

"Generous." He snatched up the container and zipped away in a huff that had Liz shaking her head.

"Is it my imagination, or is everyone super tense today, including my hubby?"

"Joe's worried about you."

"And Brian?"

"He wants to be part of the action, but knows he can't. Frustration's seeping through the cracks."

"Must be a lot of cracks. Did you tell Joe about the note?"

"No, but ask a little louder next time, and he'll hear the news from someone in this office." Angel set her palms flat on her desk. "I didn't get a note," she stage-whispered back. "Remember?"

Liz bent in from the other direction. "The walls can't talk, and you, me and Brian are pretty much the last people here." Then she straightened and fanned the computer disks like playing cards. "Look, the paperwork's done, the dead guy's been viewed, Joe's working late, and my new nanny's settling in nicely, so if you're up to it, I'm in the mood for a girl's night out. You can tell me all about sexy Noah Graydon and why you didn't sneak a peek when you had the chance." Reaching, over, she snagged a strand of Angel's hair. "You can also remind me why I'm going along with this nutso let's-not-tell-anyone-I've-been-threatened idea of yours, because I think it's suicidal. The only reason I agreed… Oh, what now?" She regarded the ringing cell phone on her belt. "Aunt Trudy. Of course."

"Another Cornish hen cremated?" Angel guessed.

"Joe mentioned that, huh?" Liz rubbed an absent thumb over her belt buckle, let her voice mail take the message "Angel, I really wish…" She halted when the phone beeped at her. "Great. Now my battery's dying. We need to talk about this threat. If not tonight, then tomorrow. Deal?"

"Do I have a choice?"

Liz tweaked her chin. "Go home, bolt in, stay safe. And eat something wholesome," she called back as she left.

It took Angel another full hour to clear off her desk and deal with her e-mails. Liz was long gone by then, and she couldn't find Brian anywhere. Maybe he'd had a date after all.

The office complex was a reconstruction, old and charming outside in keeping with the area, but a techno lover's dream behind the façade. The underground lot where they parked was another story.

Angel thought of it as a concrete cave, except the walls were streaked with exhaust, the ceiling pipes dripped and, considering it was attached to a federal building, the street people who somehow teleported in often appeared to outnumber the Feds two to one.

Okay, that was an exaggeration, but caves, concrete or otherwise, made her squeamish. Fortunately, even parking lots needed some TLC from time to time. Crews were currently acid-washing the filthy floors and walls. No one would be leaving their vehicle down there for at least another month.

Not the worst problem, in Angel's eyes. She, Brian and a handful of other people had rented spaces in a nearby alley, behind an innocuous law firm staffed by even more innocuous legalites who drifted in and out at all hours.

Liz suspected them of dealing. Brian envisioned a second floor brimming with weapons. But the number one attorney had handled Bergman's divorce, and was therefore off-limits to investigation.

Angel glanced into several of the offices she passed, but they were all empty. So, first she'd met a dead man with sockets for eyes, and now she was alone in a building that resembled a mortuary. It almost made her miss her underground parking spot.

Unwilling to speculate on what she might encounter outside, she turned her mind to the file Brian had compiled for her.

The first victim, the dead soccer mom from Danvers, had been killed eight years ago. No apparent motive; no reported dysfunction in her family life.

The second victim, a corporate lawyer like Foret, had died three months later. Unlike Foret, she had no connection to the State Department and very little on her legal plate when she died.

The CEO had two grown children, a wife who'd passed away of ovarian cancer a year earlier and a financial portfolio that had correlated perfectly with his annual salary.

The biotech had lived with his mother and sister. They'd owned a bakery and watched Bruins games together whenever possible.

The list continued in that same vein. Murdered people, living quiet, relatively uneventful lives. Married, single, male, female, young, middle-aged and old, all they appeared to have in common was a sliced carotid artery on the left side of their necks, a cryptic note and two strategically placed coins.

Except for the fifth victim, a Boston-based marketing director, and the sixth, a cop.

Angel ran contemplative fingers over her shoulder strap. In both of those cases, the personal and professional lives had been normal enough, but the pennies that should have been on the victims' eyelids had been discovered some distance away, and several of the secondary slashes had gone bone deep. Also, the cop had had a stab wound to his stomach. Interestingly enough, it was a wound that hadn't bled.

"Like our John Doe dealer," she murmured to the rear alleyway door.

Prepared for the weather, she used her security card on the lock, gave the bar a shove and stepped outside.

The wind had picked up since early evening. Sheets of newspaper flew across the pavement. She pictured the last nanny being blown away in *Mary Poppins* and grinned. Thank heaven for Walt Disney.

Reality hit when she rounded the corner. Graffiti adorned the blackened brick wall to her left. Garbage bags, split and spilling over, slumped against them. She heard traffic whizzing past on Washington, but from where Angel stood, the darkness felt oppressive, and any number of creatures, rodent and or human, could be hiding among those bags.

She debated for a moment, then relented and reached for her cell. Noah answered on the first ring.

"So you're not avoiding me after all."

She gave the phone a puzzled stare. "Excuse me, why would I avoid you?"

"Note, Angel, one you don't want Bergman to hear about."

"I had a federal friend examine the paper and print. It came back clean and empty. Anyway, I'd rather not argue right now. I'm in an alley, I'm alone, and if you tell me that's really stupid, I'll agree with you."

"Saves time. Why?"

"Am I alone in an alley?" She regarded one of the larger heaps in mild suspicion, but saw nothing except soggy bags and possibly a family of rats foraging under them. "Because I got absorbed in my work, and Brian Pinkney left the office when I wasn't looking. On the flip side, it isn't raining, and rodents, no matter how large, don't go around attacking federal agents."

"Lots of different rodents out there, Angel."

"I was going for a positive spin, Graydon. Fifty yards, and I'm at my car. I'm also armed."

"Self-sufficient to the max, and yet you called me."

"Okay, your point. Think of yourself as the TV a person turns on for company when he or she is alone in a big house and there's a storm raging outside."

"You're not exactly feeding my ego, Agent Carter."

"You're not the kind of person who needs it." She sidestepped a blob of congealed food, felt something land on her head and held up a palm. "Oh good. It's starting to rain. Forty yards."

He made a halfway amused sound. "Do me a favor and use the underground lot tomorrow."

"Can't. It's having an acid bath."

"Then leave at a decent time."

"That's a promise." The skin on her neck prickled. Her own nerves or someone in the alley?

With the rain falling more heavily, Angel could no longer separate trash cans from shadows.

To divert herself, she said, "Noah, did you know that three of the first seven victims visited the Crystal Room on a regular basis?"

"Yeah, to have their fortunes told. Another was a regular at the Tremont Tearoom."

"Three out of seven's not bad as links go."

"I agree, but this one dead-ended."

"They got their readings from different psychics?"

"No, same one, but she checked out clean, and her reputation's impeccable. Character witnesses are knee deep."

A smile stole across Angel's lips even as a fresh series of prickles started up on her neck. "Don't you love the word impeccable? Kind of sounds like unsinkable."

His chuckle helped. Ten yards to her car, she judged, though it was difficult to be sure through the now streaming rain.

"This should get me over my cave phobia."

"You're afraid of dark places?"

"Winged mammals." She squinted into the gloom, spotted her rear fender and breathed out in relief. "Made it." She beeped the fob, watched her rear lights double flash. "Car's unarmed. What was the psychic's name? It wasn't in Brian's condensed file."

"It wouldn't be. She's the former governor's sister-in-law."

Angel laughed. "There's a shock." Then considered. "Maybe that's the connection. All of the victims could be tied to a political figure—and I'll bet you already looked into that, didn't you?"

"From every conceivable angle, but the theory's holding which makes it worth another look."

"Liz hasn't been threatened, if you can call that note I got an actual threat."

"Threat, warning, it's a moot point."

Opening the driver's door, Angel tossed her bag onto the passenger seat. She was sliding into the car when she spotted movement. It came from behind, so she only caught a glimpse in her peripheral vision.

Before she could turn, hands snaked out of the blackness. They tangled in her hair and yanked. She reacted on instinct, twisting around and planting a foot in her assailant's hip.

The rain on the roof sounded like a drum. Tears of pain pricked her eyelids. Her assailant yanked again, then used his other hand to knock her backward across the stick shift.

She managed to free her gun. Half prone, she planted her foot again, this time in his pelvis, and shoved. He lost his grip on her hair, staggered backward. Angel pulled her gun arm from under the steering wheel and scrambled out of the vehicle.

He'd had a knife shoved through his belt. A foldaway knife with a nicked blade and possibly some other small marks.

She crouched on the pavement, thought she

heard something squeal when she shifted her foot. The wind gusted up, became a roar in her head. Rain pelted her. Where had he gone?

She scoured the darkness but couldn't make out the far side of the alley. She wondered if her attacker had gone under the car.

She got her answer a second later when he dove sideways across the trunk and sent her sprawling. But the pavement was slippery, and as she fell, so did he.

Angel thought it was a man. The figure moved like one, but the black outdoor gear and ski mask made identification out of the question.

Regaining her feet, she spun, double-handed her gun. Her assailant rolled and endeavored to hook her ankle. She evaded the snare, but as before, landed on something that squealed—and in this case, darted.

The rain all but blinded her. And she couldn't hear a thing when the wind whooshed down from above.

With her arm, she swiped the hair from her face. Where was he now? She combed the patchy darkness, searching for the slightest movement.

And there it was, directly ahead.

Gauging the distance, she surged up and went for his knee with a side kick that should have disabled him. Would have if she hadn't been knocked aside and into the brick wall.

Her brain wanted to fog, but she wouldn't let it. Were there two of them?

Doggedly determined, she set her sights on the

blurred motion. A growl underscored the wind. Zeroing in on it, Angel flipped her gun around back to front, ran forward and used the butt end on the man's neck.

What had been controlled motion became a frantic flurry. An elbow caught her near the top of her shoulder. Unbalanced, and not braced for the lateral assault, she stumbled, collided with something and would have ended up in the trash bags if a pair of hands hadn't intercepted her downward flight.

Okay, definitely two people.

Without the benefit of a street lamp, Angel couldn't make out the shape of the man in front of her. But she saw the knife well enough. It slashed the air in a vicious warning, then vanished.

Disentangling, she spun and took aim at the second man who'd gone to one knee on the ground.

"Don't move."

He remained on the ground for several seconds before pushing slowly back to his feet.

She maintained her stance ten feet in front of him. "All I have to do is drop my sights six inches, and you'll be minus a kneecap. Do not move."

She thought he looked winded. Or injured. It was difficult to tell with the wind blowing grit in her eyes and something close to ice pellets chattering off her hands.

"Who are you?" she demanded. "And what were you doing with the knife guy?"

"Trying to stop him, Angel."

Eyes closing in disbelief, she gave a fatalistic half-laugh, dropped her arms and regarded the sky. She no longer cared that the rain stung her cheeks and numbed her fingers. "I don't believe this." Her adrenaline-induced energy rush dissolved. "Noah, what in God's name are you doing here?"

Chapter Six

Although he was far from clear, Angel saw him rub the back of his neck. Had she hit him with her gun? She winced. "Really bad day happening here."

"No argument on this side."

A beam of light cut through the alley from the top. It lasted just long enough for her to spy the gleam of blood on Noah's hand.

Startled, she shoved her gun in the pocket of her trench. "He cut you!"

"A little. It's nothing."

But the blood told a different story.

She coddled his wrist, examined it. "Where's the wound?"

"My side, and it's not bad." He trapped her fingers before she could rip his coat apart. "I promise, Angel, it's only a scratch."

What could she do but pretend to believe him? "Is he…?" She made a drifting motion.

"Gone, yeah. He stuck me, knocked you down, or tried to, then took off."

"Which way?" She made a visual circle. "There's only straight ahead, and I swear, he didn't get past me."

With his clean hand, Noah brought her head around and tipped it up. "Think Spider-Man."

She followed the brick walls as far as she could, which wasn't far in the sheeting rain, with only the distant city glow to guide her. "Try Superman, Noah. Able to access a raised fire escape in a single bound. What did he have, a rocket pack on his back?"

Noah pointed. "The ladder was down. He used it, then pulled it up and escaped across the third floor walkway between the buildings."

"Well, I feel stupid." He didn't stop her when she swung to face him. "Was it a man?"

She saw his head move, and realized why he hadn't objected to her turning. He'd drawn her under a narrow overhang, and the shadow that sliced diagonally across his body made a silhouette of his head and left shoulder. It didn't quite disguise the blood on his coat.

She stabbed a finger at his injured side. "Okay, I'm looking at that."

To her further surprise, he offered no resistance when she drew his coat apart and tugged on his T.

"Black would be your signature color. You know how to feed the mystery, Graydon, even if it's a little cliché."

She thought his lips might have curved, but that

was pure speculation, because she really couldn't see a thing.

His hair was long, that much was fact. Long, dark and dripping on her hands.

She rolled the hem of his T-shirt carefully upward, pulling it out a bit more than necessary so she could look at his stomach. Flat, lean and fit, no surprise there. Then she lost the thought and sucked in a breath.

"My God, Noah, an inch farther up and that blade would have gone through your heart."

"It's not deep."

"Lucky you." She used her sleeve to wipe away the worst of the blood. "What are you doing here?"

"What you think. Waiting for you."

"Watching out for me, you mean. Feeling stupid doesn't make me stupid."

"I was going for a positive spin."

She heard the pain he couldn't disguise and willed her hands to remain steady.

"So you knew about the parking lot and that I was the only one left inside the building before I called you. You also figure I can't take care of myself and need a bodyguard, even though, wonder of wonders, I made it through the FBI training program with no problems. Or, well, okay, a few problems, but I was expecting boot camp, not torture test from hell."

Faint amusement overrode pain. "You had Hindleman, huh?"

She inspected the stab wound, "We called him the Purple People Eater. One of the guys I trained with used to get him hot on purpose, hoping to give him a stroke. Hindleman's face went purple at least five times a day from shouting at us, but alas, no stroke and absolutely no mercy. I feel sorry for his wife."

"Don't," Noah said. "She trained him as a recruit. Six months later, she told him they were getting married. They're having a baby next October."

Angel couldn't stop the disbelieving laugh. "In eleven months."

"Between the fifteenth and the twenty-first. My money's on the seventeenth, from 1:00 p.m. to 3:00 p.m."

"Is the pool still open?"

"Far as I know."

"I'll take the tenth between 1:00 a.m. and 3:00 a.m. Babies don't come when you want them to, they come when they come, unless Mrs. People Eater goes for a C-section, which I'm thinking a woman like that won't. Noah, you need stitches." She pressed her palm firmly against the wound. "The bleeding's not going to stop on its own."

"Yeah, it will." He covered her hand with his. "No hospitals, Angel."

"Why did I know you'd say that? What about Joe?"

"I don't need stitches. What I need is for you to get in your car so I can follow you home."

She waved a hand in front of his face. "News flash, Graydon, I survived the Purple People Eater's training program. I won't pretend it was smart of me to come into this alley alone, but I promise you, I could have handled that guy. Okay, maybe not apprehended him, but lived to be really pissed off."

"And possibly stabbed."

"Possibly, but unlike you, if I'd been stabbed, I'd go to the hospital for treatment."

"As opposed to standing in the rain, bleeding."

She offered a perfunctory smile. "Your middle name's perverse, right?"

"I thought it was obtuse."

"Let's go with stubbornly difficult and move on." She thought, she hoped, the blood flow had at least slowed.

Noah wrapped his fingers around her wrist, but still didn't push her away. "Trust me, Angel, I've had worse injuries."

She didn't want to believe that. Unfortunately, like it or not, she had in fact heard the rumors about him. Badly disfigured, some people suggested. Carved up by a madman, other said. Why else would he keep to the shadows, never come to the office, never be seen? Never venture outside?

Not true in the case of the last thing, but as for the rest…

The wind continued to buffet them. Rain slanted under the awning. Noah seemed disinclined to leave. Angel certainly didn't want to. But someone had to move. Or speak. Or act.

A moment later, as if conjured by her thoughts, a second headlight sliced through the alley.

The split second shot of Noah's profile made the breath in Angel's lungs stall. The word *stunning* sprang to mind, followed by *sexy* and *sensual* and—she couldn't help it—*rock star.* Gorgeous, tall, dark-haired rock star, one who should have a gaggle of groupies trailing around behind him.

"Something?" he asked, and she knew he'd caught her staring.

She raised tentative fingers to the right side of his jaw. "Not sure. Maybe."

Did his lips twitch? Did it matter? Moving closer, she kissed his cheek. "Thank you, Noah."

"For what? Being here?"

"For knowing this could happen. For seeing what I missed. And yes, for being here. I should have realized he'd try to ambush me. The guy loves docks and alleyways."

She kissed his cheek again, but it wasn't what she wanted. She knew that, and so did he.

"You're doing it again, Angel." He set his mouth next to her temple. "I swear you're the queen of low blows."

She had to laugh, even though her skin was tingling and the blood was zinging like tiny electric bolts through her veins. "That remark has all sorts of connotations, from simple to sexual." She snuck a look at the wound beneath her fingers and was relieved to see that the bleeding had pretty much stopped. "You're more like Superman than the killer." Her eyes moved upward to the shadow that still managed to blot out most of his face. "If a thousand times more mysterious. I saw you, Noah, just for a second, and you're gorgeous. I know that sounds shallow, and as I said before, it doesn't matter to me, but you are, you're absolutely gorgeous. Why on earth…?"

It was all she got out. This time it was Noah who moved, Noah who framed her face with his hands to hold her still. Noah who murmured a regretful, "I'm going to pay for this…" And crushed his mouth onto hers.

SHE COULDN'T BREATHE, didn't even try to think. Of all the things he could have done, disappearing being at the top of the list, a full-blown, soul-stirring, openmouthed kiss hadn't numbered in Angel's top ten.

That didn't mean she couldn't respond to it, that she wouldn't happily abandon her own control and explore his mouth as thoroughly as he was exploring hers.

Her fingers curled in his wet hair. When the wind blew her forward, she went with it, pressing herself tightly enough against him that she could feel the rock-hard contours of his body.

He wanted her, that single, simple fact registered

clearly through the hot swirl of emotion in her brain. God knew she wanted him. Hadn't realized how much until this moment, but there it was, desire, hunger and need all twirling around inside, urging her to draw him over to her car and make love to him in an alley.

He used his tongue to drive her crazy. He dipped and tasted and circled until she tore her mouth away. Partly for air, but perhaps for something else as well. Because she couldn't have formed a rational thought if she'd wanted to. And she was trying, even as she sank her teeth into his bottom lip.

Her breath came in spurts, like the kisses she feathered from cheek to ear. She nipped the lobe, then let her head fall back as he ran his lips along the side of her jaw.

Her eyes closed, her mind floated. This was so completely out there for her, such an opposite reaction to the one she usually had when a man wanted to take his kisses to the next level. But no other man had ever smelled so good, or made her feel like there was lava in her veins. No one else could or likely would taste so sinful or so hot.

She breathed his name, then snagged his hair again so she could kiss him full on the mouth, long and hard and deep.

Instinct told her he'd break it off. She was counting on it actually, because no way would she be able to end something so incredible.

"Angel." He dragged his lips from hers. "Angel, we have to stop."

"Know that." But she bit him one last time, before licking the sting. "Good thing one of us has a scrap of self-discipline."

"A microscopic scrap at this point."

She started to raise her hand to his left cheek, but he trapped her wrist and held fast. She drew back slightly, narrowed her eyes and thought maybe... she wasn't sure what.

Curiosity in the form of a light shiver danced along her spine.

"You're cold," Noah said.

"Cold outside, hot in. Noah, why can't...?"

But his lips recaptured hers for a final heart-stopping kiss and the question evaporated.

"You need to be home," he said into her mouth. "Out of the rain and away from this alley."

She sensed motion, opened her eyes and laughed in surprise when he stood back. Somehow he'd floated her across the pavement and deposited her on the seat of her car.

"Well, that was a good trick. Houdini'd have had a hard time managing—" she brought her eyes up, encountered only rain and darkness and finished with an inured "—it. Hell..."

As her mind and body cooled, Angel studied the traces of blood on her hand. Noah Graydon was nothing if not a puzzle, she reflected, one which, frankly, she might have trouble piecing together.

Except…

What was it she'd seen, or thought she'd seen right before he'd vanished? A black patch over his left eye, or a trick of the shadowy half-light?

Whatever the case, she was sure of one thing. Like Lionel Foret's murder, Noah was a mystery she fully intended to solve.

HE WAS PREPARED TO spend the night in his truck. Thankfully, the bleeding in his side had stopped.

He could have gone to Joe for stitches, but his mind was a mess right now, and Joe knew how to read his moods. One look and he'd see trouble in the form of an Angel.

A light burned in her bedroom until well past midnight. Noah watched the glow through half-closed eyes, fought to keep his mind on the present and not let it stray to the alley where she'd been attacked.

The take-out coffee he'd ordered had a bitter edge, like the memory of his opponent's escape. Losing the guy had pissed him off big time. That was twice he'd been outmaneuvered, although admittedly, tonight he'd been more concerned with keeping Angel safe than in apprehending a killer.

As a result, he'd wound up kissing her, damn near making out with her, not five minutes after she'd almost been sliced up by a madman.

Noah deflected the horror of that thought by re-calling the feel of Angel's mouth on his. Gorgeous, she'd called him, and the memory brought a wry smile to his lips. Not exactly what he'd wanted to hear, but then he'd given up trying to figure out what he wanted to hear, maybe needed to hear, a long time ago.

Vanity wasn't his burden. Yeah, he was guilty of it, but not to the point of arrogance, and never, he hoped, at the cost of another person's life.

Still, the weight of his thoughts now was nothing compared to the weight of guilt in his mind as memory shifted from tonight's alley to a waterfront warehouse five years ago.

The light in Angel's bedroom winked out, distracting him. Noah finished his coffee, slouched deeper into his seat. And hoped like hell the killer would show.

THE DARK HOURS WENT ON forever. Day, night, it made no difference. Darkness was a state of mind now, and failure left a bitter taste, even when it came on the heels of success.

Yesterday's victim had been an unexpected coup, an achievement on two fronts. Killing him should have been enough to sate, or at least soothe, until the real target could be dispatched. But the real target had eluded death again, turning satisfaction to fury. Worse, she'd been aided by the person who'd made her a target in the first place.

Now, that was irony at its loathsome best. But

defeat was never easy to swallow and anger even more difficult to dispel.

Belief would make it happen, though. Five years of waiting, of holding the anger in, of redirecting it was about to end. Had ended. Death was once more making its statement, leaving its mark, doing its job.

When it was over, Angel would be gone and Noah would be devastated. Mission complete.

Almost...

"I CALL HIM THE DOUGH-BOY," Joe said a few days later. "No disrespect intended, Noah, but the guy was flabby and soft. Big, yes, but I'd guess slow to react."

"You still going with a copycat killing?"

"Makes the most sense, to me..." Joe's suddenly preoccupied gaze traveled across the restaurant he'd chosen as a meeting place. "I wonder if he's the one?"

In the back of the booth, Noah propped his booted foot on a chair and let the shadows do their job. He could ask his friend the obvious question, but why bother when he already knew the answer. He'd seen Pete Peloni at Angel's place on Thursday night. Pete and his female passenger. Anything he said at this point would only send Joe off on a paranoid bent.

He'd spent a cramped and thankfully uneventful night staring at Angel's bedroom window. Fantasizing a little? Oh, yeah—and a lot more than a little. Thing was, he felt more tuned in to his surroundings this morning than he had in years. No way would the killer get her. Him, possibly. Her, not a chance.

Joe's fingers on the table kept time to Green Day while he trailed the restaurant owner's movements around the large room. "Some guy named Pete left a message on our machine last night, Noah. Don't know why I checked. Anything important goes to voice mail on my cell. But there was this message for Liz, and I heard it, and the only Pete I could think of was Peloni, and I only know the name because Angel told me he makes the best healthy eats in town."

"Angel eats health food?"

"Only when forced—which Liz and her mother do as often as possible." Joe's sandy brows came together. "Why would Peloni phone my wife?"

Half-lidded, Noah watched Pete assist an elderly woman into a chair. "What did the message say?"

"'Sorry to call you at home. We need to talk.'"

"Maybe he has some information for her."

"Uh-huh." Joe's eyes returned to the man in the green denim shirt. "Why not call Angel? She's the one he has the hots for."

Noah's gaze grew contemplative. Then slid sideways to his friend's worried face. "Liz isn't cheating, Joe. She doesn't have the capacity for it."

Concern teamed up with exasperation. "You've never even met her. How can you possibly know what her capacity is?"

"You profile criminals for a living, your instincts tend to kick in all over the place." Noah unzipped his jacket. He'd showered and changed earlier, but he still felt edgy after last night, with the memory of Angel's mouth heating his blood and a makeshift bandage covering the gash in his side. "Call it a hunch in the case of your wife, and ask her about the message."

"I guess." Joe picked up the menu, tried to shake his mind clear. "I'm ravenous this morning in any case. I did two full autopsies last night—not the Doe-boy—and today I'm giving a pep talk to a group of med students who are thinking about going into forensics."

"It wasn't a copycat."

Joe blinked, stared. "Are you serious? Why not? That stab wound…"

"Was for show."

Joe's frown deepened. "It was inflicted after death, that's true, but what about the pennies, or lack thereof? And some of those slashes were positively amateurish. By that I mean it's as if the murderer got lucky hitting the carotid artery. There were at least five other good-sized cuts on the guy's neck."

"Inflicted before or after death?"

"Well, okay, after for the most part, but even a cover-up's atypical, isn't it? And then there's the big Kahuna, the missing eyes. Now that's something our boy's never done before. And, yes, the damage was done after death, but that would be a given no matter who the killer was."

"Old story, new twist. Remember the cop six years ago and the marketing director before him? Cop was stabbed after death. And there were other inconsistencies."

Perplexed, Joe scratched the back of his neck. "I don't know how your mind works, Noah, and I probably wouldn't understand if you told me, so I'll just accept what you're saying and simply ask why. Why would the guy change his MO for two murders, revert back to his original style, take five years off, then start the whole process again? First murder consistent with several of the previous ones, second, a complete aberration. Is he trying to throw you off, or is he just so wacko that sometimes he follows a self-written rule book and other times he decides to hell with it and tosses the book in the toilet?"

Resting an elbow on the shelf beside him, Noah ran the side of his index finger under his lower lip. He almost missed the question as he recalled Angel's body pressed against his, but caught enough of it to move a shoulder. "I'll let you know when I figure it out. In the meantime, take it on faith. John Doe's death wasn't a copycat."

"Hey there, X-Man," a new voice cut in. "Long time, yadda yadda."

Noah dropped his hand. "Pete." He made a head motion between the two men. "Joe, this is Pete Peloni. Pete…"

"Call me X-Man Two," Joe inserted. "Number One's partner in crime so to speak."

Pete had a hearty laugh, and he used it on them. "So now I've got a pair of X-Men on my list of patrons. A pair of X's, a handful of G's and one guy who wants me to believe he's Secret Service, but who is in fact a salesman for a prosthetics company."

"Six Million Dollar Man," Noah remarked and earned another laugh.

"Okay, gentlemen, breakfast special's twelve grain flapjacks with Quebec maple syrup, a fresh local berry compote, honey-lime yogurt and my signature granola mix. Otherwise," he winked at Noah, "the Eggs Benny's great, and the New England Sampler always sells like—well, hotcakes."

"I'll go for jacks," Joe said. "My wife," he gave the word a subtle emphasis, "wants me to spruce up my eating habits. For the sake of the kids."

"Smart wife." Pete grinned at Noah. "Let me guess. The Sampler?"

"Sounds good."

"Twenty minutes if you want those coffees topped. Or you can switch to green tea."

At six feet tall, Pete had no height advantage on Joe, or much muscle mass either, since Liz and her husband worked out regularly together. The hair was another matter. Pete had enough for a thick, curly ponytail, while Joe moaned that his was growing sparser by the day.

When the owner disappeared into the kitchen Noah arched a brow. "Verdict?"

"Too cheerful." Grimacing, Joe touched a cautious palm to the top of his head. "It puts people off first thing in the morning."

Noah glanced around the bustling restaurant. "Not sure that's true, but then we deal in death on a daily basis. The general population might have a less jaded attitude."

"And I might be reading too much into a phone message." Joe made the reluctant concession, then revved up again and aimed a finger at the kitchen door. "It was his voice, though, on her machine, so he did call my wife. And don't give me that look, Noah. You wouldn't like it if he called Angel."

"I wouldn't know if he called Angel, and you're acting like a jealous husband. Steer back to forensic pathology and talk to me about John Doe. His eyes were gouged rather than removed, right?"

"Definitely gouged, and with a very rough hand."

"What about the artery?"

"We've been through this, Noah. It was the same as the others, a clean slice. This killer's all over the map, which brings me back to the word of the day—wacko. How do you profile someone like that?"

"You get into his head. You become."

Concern immediately spread across Joe's features. "That sounds dangerous."

"Only if the becoming takes hold."

"As in you lose yourself in the part?"

"It happens."

"But not to you."

"No."

"What about Prune—er, Bill Skater?"

Noah shrugged. "Might get lost in his office, but that's about it."

"Floor-to-ceiling mess. It's a miracle he can find anything, let alone figure out what a murderer's thinking." Then, "What is he thinking, Noah? What's his point? The victims are so diverse it's like he's pulling names out of a hat. Or some online phone book."

"Superiority complex."

"Excuse me?"

"He's better than us, or thinks he is. Better, wiser, craftier."

"Wisdom plays into this?"

"He wants his actions to be recognized. His cause is noble. His messages prove that."

"He slashes a major artery. How can that be noble?"

"I said his messages, not his method."

"Are we talking full-blown nut ball here?" When Noah slanted him a look, Joe spread his hands. "Hey, I went the way of forensics, not psychiatry. Explain to a lowly death doctor how a bloodthirsty lunatic can feel superior, smart or noble."

"When I can, I will. In the meantime…" Noah's

mind slid sideways to Angel before he dragged it back. "Take me through it, Joe, slash by slash. Tell me what was done to the latest victim before he died, and what came after."

Joe nodded. "All right, despite my reservations, I'll go through it again and help you become. But then I'm going to ask for a favor in return."

"You want me to check out Peloni."

"Right down to the brand of underwear he likes. And who, if anyone, buys it for him. Okay, that sounds obsessive, but I've got a lot on my mind right now. Not just Liz and this new round of murders that I still don't think she and Angel should have been asked to take on, but Graeme, too. He's not himself, and that's a concern. He hasn't been out with a woman since last Friday."

"Joe, it's Monday. We're only talking two days here."

"No, I mean a week ago this past Friday. That's nine days or more. Now come on, nine days without sex for Graeme is like nine years for the rest of us... Er, am I treading on sensitive ground here?"

"I'll let you know if you cross a line."

"You don't think I should be worried?"

"Not until he hits a month."

"What about Liz and...?" He flapped a hand at the kitchen.

"I'll look, but for my money, the answer's no."

"Why don't I feel better hearing that?"

"Because worry's a state of mind for you."

"She's holding something back, Noah, I'm not wrong. I also know it could be work-related, and that's fair enough. But the Graeme thing's just plain weird. I mean, come on, nine days? I'm telling you, when we were in high school…"

Careful not to jar his healing ribs, Noah sat back and let his friend reminisce. Half of his mind listened. The other half wandered in Angel's direction.

Very bad idea, he reflected, and even worse control for a man who prided himself on his ability to block out any and all distractions in favor of his work. Maybe Joe had crossed a line after all, and in doing so exposed what would have been better left buried.

A couple rose from the table to his right. The man tossed his newspaper onto the shelf between booths. Noah wouldn't have given it a second thought if two words from the headline hadn't leaped out at him: "Penny Killer".

Reaching over, he spun the top section around. Joe had segued from high school to med school on memory lane. Both his and the background voices became a buzz in Noah's head.

The newspaper article was extensive, five half-page columns. It talked about Lionel Foret and John Doe. It also touched on a similar round of murders that had stopped suddenly after the death of an FBI rookie.

Noah scanned the column, picked out key words and phrases. Then he picked out the name of the reporter who'd written them.

Paul Reuben.

Chapter Seven

"It's the worst possible nightmare. I was young when I had him, only sixteen." In Lionel Foret's topsy-turvy North End condo, Joy Foret Smith wiped her narrow cheeks with a damp tissue. "Even so, you give birth to a child, you figure he'll bury you, not the other way around."

Angel touched her hand. "I don't know what it is to lose a child, Ms. Smith. All I can say is that we'll find the person who murdered your son and make him pay some kind of price for what he's done."

The woman peered at her through a pair of large, round glasses that swallowed up more than half her face. She was small-boned, almost painfully thin and reminded Angel strongly of a mantis.

"He was a good boy," she insisted. Anger butted against sorrow to create puffy-eyed indignation. "He had a canary, for heaven's sake. My boyfriend keeps a tarantula, and my son keeps a Tweety Bird."

A tarantula? "Your son sounds very nice," Angel

agreed. "Ms. Smith, if my partner and I are going to apprehend the person who murdered him, we need to know whether there was anyone in his life who wasn't quite so nice."

When the woman removed her glasses, her eyes virtually disappeared. She peered nearsightedly at Angel. "I went over this with your boss the day I arrived in Boston. There was no one, not a soul. Even his old girlfriends liked him."

Liz positioned her pen over an open notebook. "Do you have names?"

"Certainly." She put the glasses back on, blinked her re-magnified eyes and searched through her purse. "I made up a list. Names, addresses, phone numbers. I've talked to every one of them since Lionel's death, and they all plan to attend the memorial service in Washington. He had no enemies, Agent Thomas." Played out, she shrank into herself. "His mother, yes, but not Lionel." Then she puffed up a little. "He went to school with our Secretary of State, you know."

"Yes, we heard that." Angel would have paced if the living room hadn't been crammed with newspapers and magazines. One bump and the stacks would topple like dominoes.

So she remained on the arm of the sofa beside Foret's grieving mother and forced herself to think without benefit of motion—think about the case, she reminded herself, not about Noah as she'd done all last night and most of this morning.

She unbuttoned her dark chocolate leather coat. "Is it possible that someone with a grudge against you might have gone after your son out of spite?"

Joy shook her head. "When I said enemies, Agent Carter, I meant people I've annoyed in some way over the years. Disgruntled neighbors, maybe an old in-law or two. I tend to do that to people without meaning to. Two years ago, I had to testify in court regarding a coworker's unethical behavior, but the judge found me irritating. In the end, the coworker got off with a slap and a transfer that actually worked out well for him. There was another man, as well—not a coworker—who stole cars and stripped them down to the frames. I really shouldn't have crossed him. He was a mean one."

"Was he also a vengeful one?" Liz inquired.

Joy gave a watery laugh. "Possibly, but as it turned out, he had nothing to avenge." She took Angel's hand in her claw-like fingers. "Here's the story. Once upon a time, last summer to be precise, there was this dispatcher, a little long in the tooth, say fifty-eight, who felt she had the stuff to be a detective. One day, opportunity knocked, and she simply couldn't resist the challenge. But she lost her cool, blundered in solo and wound up ruining a sting that had been two months in the making. Her captain was livid, because in the end, the mark—aka the car thief—walked, with a smile on his face and a flip of his middle finger. Cut to the happy ending? For all his mad, the captain was a decent guy. No reprimand for the bumbling dispatcher, even though the car thief had the balls to send the department a thank you card."

The woman's grip was clammy, but Angel let her hold on. "It's an interesting story. But you're right, no reason for the thief to harbor a grudge."

Joy's shoulders drooped. "I'd say more humiliating than interesting. The card he sent came with a five-pound box of Godiva chocolates and a rose for every female in the department. No grudge, no detective's badge, and nothing I seem to be able to do to help you solve my son's murder."

"Something will turn up." Recalling her encounter in the alley last night, Angel covered a chill with a smile. "I don't believe your son's death was a random act, Ms. Smith. I do believe that with every day that passes we get closer to the murderer."

The level look Liz shot her suggested otherwise, however, she said nothing while Foret's mother gathered up her son's Tweety-Bird cage—almost as tall as she was—and left to thank the neighbor who'd been feeding him. The moment the door closed, she flipped her notebook shut. "Angel…"

"I always liked Sylvester better than Tweety, didn't you?"

Liz glared. "You lied to that woman."

Standing, Angel pressed her knuckle into a damp flowerpot. "I made her feel better, Liz. And, I *was* close to the murderer last week. I hit him with my gun." She replayed the incident, rubbed her knuckle clean. "I hope."

"To which he responded by stabbing Noah Graydon instead of you. In the biz, we call that pure dumb luck, and face it, Angel, that's all it was. Three of you in a dark alley. No one knows who's who."

"Noah and the killer knew who I was." Though she probably shouldn't have pointed that out.

Liz stuffed the notebook in her jacket pocket. "Well, hurrah for half a good thing. You should have called me. I'd have come back."

"All the way from New Bedford?"

"Where?"

Angel searched for her car keys on the sofa. "Your Aunt Trudy lives in New Bedford, right? You spent the weekend there."

"Aunt Tru… Oh, yes she does, and I did. But it's possible I was only en route when you left. Anyway, if not me, you could have called Noah."

"We've been through this, Liz. I did call Noah." Spinning the found key ring on her finger, Angel headed for the door. She wouldn't let her mind go back to the moment, wouldn't dwell or obsess. They'd kissed. She'd dreamed. Okay, dreamed every night since then, but he had an incredible mouth. What normal, healthy woman wouldn't have trouble getting a scene like that out of her head? "Are you coming?"

"Coming, but I'm not shutting up."

Angel set her hip against the doorframe. "Noah was already there, Liz, watching out for me."

"Which is just more dumb luck on your part. You've been threatened by a very elusive, highly successful serial killer. I don't care how well trained you are, you're in danger… And I hate keeping secrets."

There it was, the crux of the conversation. "You want me to tell Bergman."

"Or let me tell Joe. Please, Angel, let me talk to him."

"I—" Liz's request surprised a frown out of her. "Why?"

"Because he's my husband, and keeping secrets from your spouse is wrong."

A bubble of amusement formed. "Uh, Liz, we're FBI. We have an inexhaustible supply of secrets, many of which can't be told, even to husbands. Mine's simply another on that lengthy list."

Her partner huffed out a breath, took a last look around the messy living room. "I'm not going to argue about this, partner, but I still think you shouldn't be keeping that threat to yourself. And don't say you're not, because for all intents and purposes, you damn well are."

Angel's lips quirked. "Wrong side of the bed this morning, huh?"

"Maybe. Yes." Liz pushed at her hair, struggled to unruffle. "I haven't been sleeping well. The weekend was only so-so. My aunt's having a memory problem. And we've been working a lot of late nights, mostly in the lab for Joe, but sometimes at the Victims' Support Center where we volunteer. We hardly see each other anymore. To top it off, Graeme dropped in for breakfast this morning. He looked like hell, acted weird and bailed while I was making him hot cereal."

"Maybe he had a date." Angel pressed the light switch, pulled Liz through the door. "Or got an emergency page from the hospital."

"His clothes were rumpled, Angel."

That got her attention. "Graeme? Our Graeme's clothes were rumpled?"

"Thought that'd shock you. He was untidy, untucked and unshaved. In other words, about as un-Graeme-like as he could be."

"Okay… Huh." Puzzled, Angel snicked the deadbolt. "Maybe he…" Then she felt something against her ankle and glanced down. "Oh, perfect, just what this place needs, more newspapers. Where did these come from?"

"Doorman's been collecting them. He must have brought them up for Foret's mother. Subscriptions are paid to the end of the year on three different papers. Twice daily delivery, it adds up."

"Apparently." Angel angled her gaze as a headline in one of the less reputable publications caught her eye. "Look at this, Liz." She circled for a better view and bent to read from the pile. "'Penny Killer's

Bloodbath Continues.' It's an article about Foret." A slow smile worked its way across her lips. "And John Doe."

Uninterested at first, Liz did a slow about-face. "An article about someone we haven't confirmed as one of the victims yet? Oh, let me guess. Gotta be Paul Reuben's byline, right?"

"You get the stuffed bear." As she scanned the print, a wicked light sparked Angel's eyes. "From the look of his article, partner, this byline just shot Mr. Reuben to the top of our extremely short suspect list."

AFTER A BRIEF ARGUMENT, they agreed to split up. Liz took the reporter's poolroom haunts, Angel did the bars, or planned to, after a detour.

Reuben worked in a dingy downtown building that had her thinking Gotham City as she boarded the clunky, cage-style elevator. If she'd had more time, she would have used the stairs, but twenty-three flights would have been a challenge for Batman, never mind someone who'd gotten less than three hours of sleep last night.

"Okay, stop right there," she cautioned herself as the elevator jittered upward. "Fantasies about sexy FBI profilers not permitted."

Despite the building's gloomy aspect, the newsroom was a typical, if somewhat constricted, workspace. The chief editor's office was the only one actually sealed off top and sides. Computer keys tapped in the surrounding cubbies, printers whirred, and no fewer than a dozen phones rang at once.

It came as no surprise to Angel that Reuben's editor had a cynical attitude, a lip that looked permanently curled, and a dribble of coffee down the front of his shirt. Smiles didn't charm him and subtle threats only deepened his sneer. He dismissed her after five minutes, then dropped the blind on his door as a parting insult when she left.

More amused than offended, Angel started back to the elevator. It would take a jerk to run a rag like this. A little more polish, a lot less sleaze, and Paul Reuben could have ditched the place for a far more respectable job.

He knew better than most how to get there first, was a master at milking a story and had the how-to of careful wording down to an art.

Still, she had to wonder how he could possibly have learned about John Doe's connection to the Penny Killer when the only people who believed a connection even existed would never have considered talking.

A small part of her hoped Reuben would turn out to be the killer, but that was a mean thought and not really how she expected it to go. Still, you never knew about people. Dirty little skeletons emerged from the most surprising closets, and Paul Reuben struck her as a man who'd have more than a few skeletons.

She'd almost made it through the maze of cubby walls when someone marched around a corner and halted her with palm slapped to her shoulder.

Janis Joplin was Angel's first thought. Not necessarily straight, was her second. The woman's hair hung in frizzy tails beneath a black bandana. Her teeth and fingers said she'd been smoking forever, and at 3:00 p.m., she already smelled strongly of beer.

"No cracks," she warned in a rusty Janis voice. "No judgments, no bull. You're FBI, and I hate Paul Reuben."

"Must be awfully thin glass in your editor's office walls," Angel noted. "Yes, I am FBI, I don't make snap judgments and you can drop the hand, I'm listening."

"Just so you know, I make it a point not to screw with feds or cops. But Reuben's screwed me around more than once, so I'm going to help you out. Brogan's Farm."

Angel waited, but she didn't elaborate. "Could you be more specific? I've only lived in Boston for eighteen months."

The woman made a grunting sound. "It's a farm north of here. Old man Brogan does a huge pumpkin smash every year between Halloween and Thanksgiving. People bring their rotting jack-o'-lanterns and sledge them to a pulp."

"Sounds like a great outlet for pent-up brutality."

"We call it an exorcism of kinetic anger in our

write-ups. Who needs therapy when you can splat a pumpkin's head? Kids love it better than Wii."

"Again, great. Can we get back to Paul Reuben?"

"Brogan's his first ex-father-in-law. Reuben's at the farm helping the old man keep things in order. Might be working with the turkeys as well."

"Which will subsequently be sledged and purchased for Thanksgiving dinner by the pumpkin smashers."

"You're pretty bright for a pretty woman."

"Thank you." Angel arched a brow. "Directions?"

"I'll draw you a map."

She tried to call Liz as she left the city, but the line was busy so she left a detailed voice mail. Another fifteen miles and she'd be there. Even the weather was cooperating. The sky might be overcast, but the rain had stopped, colorful leaves skittered across the road, and if one or two thoughts of Noah snuck in to fire her blood, who needed to know about it but her?

She reached the farm by four fifteen. There was no sign of Reuben or the old man who ran the place. There were, however, scores of turkeys waddling around in front of a barn ramshackle enough to be pre-Revolution. Two tractors, almost as old, and a flatbed truck with rusty back rails and four flat tires stood like weary sentinels in front of the doors.

Might be more fun to smash the machinery, put it out of its misery, she thought, checking her gun.

A cluster of smaller buildings dotted the area. No house that she could see, but pretty much everything else a fossilized farm might need, including an outhouse toilet minus its roof.

She began with the barn, hoped the light would hold and not be swallowed up by the bank of black clouds hovering like vultures to the west. Because bats loved old barns, and she really didn't need to be freaked out when and if she located Paul.

The large door stood ajar. Wind whistled around the edge, creating a ghostly shriek that echoed through the bare center.

Shades of a Salem torture chamber, she thought, then glanced sharply skyward as something black streaked past overhead.

But it was only a crow gliding toward its rooftop perch.

Right, no jitters there. No bats either, and no way she would cave to a phobia.

Shoving her gun under her coat, Angel stepped through the door, and listened while her eyes adjusted.

She could hear the turkeys but little else—until the rafters moaned and drew her gaze to the loft.

She saw a little girl with braids and skinned knees, exploring the upper level, hoping to find a stash of straw she could spin into gold. But in the middle of the search, voices reached her from below, a man's and woman's. Within seconds, the voices were replaced by other sounds, breathy and excited. So she hunched down and waited, silent in the loft. Until…

"Stop it." Irritated with her memory for allowing even a portion of the fear in, Angel set a hand on her gun, and moved forward. "Paul," she called out. "It's Angel. Are you here?"

No response. Only an eerie clacking sound high above.

Old man Brogan, she reflected, was missing the boat by limiting himself to a yearly pumpkin smash. With very little effort, he could have worked this place into a lucrative pre-Halloween horror show. The cobwebs between loft and ladder were so heavy they'd need no enhancement. On the other hand, their presence indicated that no one had climbed that ladder for several years.

Although far from comforting, it was hardly a new thought. Angel had known from the start that this might be a setup.

The feeble light filtering through the windows began to fade. Clouds must be creeping in. She knew she should leave, but this killer needed to be caught before any more people died or—she thought of Noah and ground her teeth—were injured.

The air smelled of moldy hay, dried manure and, occasionally, when the wind reached her, the smoky remnants of a late fall bonfire.

Spying a smaller door on the side wall, she headed toward it.

The shadows lengthened; the barn grew darker. Beyond the walls, the wind picked up. The smell of burning wood and leaves grew more pronounced.

Like its big brother, the side door was ajar and rocking on arthritic hinges that protested even the smallest movement.

For Angel's money, Lionel Foret's Munster fix had nothing on this place. The dark patches altered with every shift of cloud outside, and the wind had started to rattle some of the window slats.

A plow that had to predate Paul Revere's famous ride lay tipped on its side. Its leather harness had been gnawed by mice and the body looked to be permeated by woodworms.

Could have been an artifact, she reflected while skirting it, but like the rest of the farm, it had been left to molder. Small wonder Brogan had resorted to gimmickry to make his money.

Ten feet from the door, she spotted a movement and halted.

Unsure, she went with her instinct and drew the gun from her waistband. Better to be safe and if necessary apologize to Farmer Brogan for the armed intrusion.

Barrel up, she approached the door. Beyond it, the deepest shadow reshaped itself, transforming from a disproportionate blob to something approaching a human side view.

Angel muttered a low, "If you're playing me,

Reuben, I swear to God, I'll take you in and give you to Brian for bone-grinding and bread-making."

She fixed her gaze on the crack between the hinges and counted. The shadow had gone blob-like again, but it didn't matter. She'd seen what she'd seen. Hallucinations weren't part of her makeup.

When she got to five, she sucked in a breath, used her foot to lift the wood latch and swung across the threshold. The shadow mirrored her action. As the door hit the wall, she spied the opposing gun.

Aimed right at the center of her forehead.

THREE LONG, TENSION-FILLED SECONDS passed. With a rush of breath, Angel batted the other weapon aside and lowered her arms. "I swear to God, Graydon, you really could give Lamont Cranston a run for his money."

"Supplementary training… Ah." He paused, angled up and away, then let his own hand fall.

Behind her, Angel heard a telltale crack of sound and gave the shadow in which Noah stood a questioning look. "Someone's back there with a bigger gun than yours, yeah?"

"You got it, lady," a gruff voice answered. "Now turn real slow so's I can see your hands."

"Farmer Brogan?" she assumed, following his instructions.

He touched the tip of a very large sawed off

shogun to her ribs. "That's right." In near darkness, the man's expression bordered on evil. "Too bad for you, I'm the kind of farmer who doesn't take kindly to trespassers."

Chapter Eight

To Angel's relief, Brogan's mean was primarily for show. His shotgun, she discovered, wasn't even loaded. Twenty minutes and a lengthy explanation later, he was sufficiently satisfied to indicate a billow of smoke rising over a distant hillock.

"Fella you're wanting's down in the hollow. Make sure you got your stomach in order before you go hunting him down. You as well," he said to Noah behind her.

He tromped back into the barn, leaving Angel to marvel at Noah's ability to remain a figure of mystery even in the face of an illegal weapon.

But the admiration was secondary to more pressing questions. She sent him a serene smile. "Okay. How, when, why?"

"Had no idea you were here. Fifteen minutes ago. I got a tip."

His last answer took her smile from serene to sparkling. "Did your tipster happen to bear a striking resemblance to Janis Joplin?"

"More like Elvira at seventy. I went to the Crystal Room. Reuben's into psychic readings."

"Or claims he is when in pursuit of a lead." Amusement ebbed. "You realize, Noah, that if you want to talk to him, which I assume you do since you apparently read the same article as I did, you'll need to come out of the shadows to do it."

"Or I could let you do it and just get your back."

She could almost see him. She could definitely feel him. Something in the air between them felt charged, like the promise of electrifying sex with no taboos.

She took a step closer. "Don't you think it's time we quit playing hide-and-seek?"

Already leaning against a tree stump, he held his hands out to the sides. "Not stopping you, Agent Carter."

She should be looking for Paul Reuben. But Angel knew it was one of her failings that her priorities occasionally got skewed.

The shadows seemed to swirl around them. But then the last rays of afternoon light did her a favor and danced across his features. Right side first—gorgeous as before—then the left. And seeing, really seeing for the first time, she thought maybe, just maybe, she understood.

"You do wear an eye patch." Although close enough to touch now, she made no move to do so. Was that a scar on the upper part of his left cheek, or a trick of the dying light? Whatever it was, her heart hurt for him, and for whatever had made him think he needed to conceal himself in a world of darkness.

Because he was still incredibly gorgeous. Pirate meets rock star, she decided. She started to lift her hand, but stopped when he caught and trapped her fingers.

Despite his reaction, a sense of amazement shimmered through her. She was seeing him, actually looking at his face for the very first time. In its own way, and in this strange setting, the experience felt vaguely surreal, not at all the way she'd imagined it would be.

A smile tugged on her lips. "You've got style, Noah, I'll give you that." Because she couldn't brush his cheek, she brought the back of his hand to hers. "And when it's all said and done, you don't disappoint."

HE COULD HAVE PUT her off, could have remained a shadow while he watched and listened and processed. But during the past week, he'd made his decision. She wanted to see him; he'd let her see him. Let her make of him what she chose.

She moved closer, tilted her head. "Brown eyes?" she guessed.

His lips quirked. "Hazel."'

"Bet they're pure gold in the sun."

"If you're a romantic."

"I have my moments." Clearly regretful, she set her free hand on his chest, gave it a pat. "I could get lost in you, Graydon, but Paul Reuben knows things he shouldn't, and we need to figure out why before more people die."

He lifted the fingers of the hand he still held to his lips, gave them a quick kiss. "There'll be better moments."

"I imagine Reuben's going to feel the same way."

Noah could tell she wanted to see more, wanted to pull him into what remained of the light. But with Hindleman's training prodding her, she squared her shoulders and set her sights on the hillock. "He'd better have some good answers for us."

"Oh, he'll have answers." Noah angled his hat over his patched left eye, pushed off from the stump. "The trick will be for us to determine if they're true or false." He lowered his mouth to her ear. "And if he's doing what we assume he's doing down in that hollow, not to wind up in the same condition as his current victims."

WITH THE DARKNESS CAME a natural cover for Noah. Beyond the perimeter of an enormous bonfire, shadows hung like a thick black mantle. He fell back slightly as they approached the reporter who was seated on a wooden stool, tossing turkey parts into a wheelbarrow.

"Who snitched?" he demanded, not looking up.

Angel noticed another stool, dusted off the top

and sat. "How did you put it the last time we met? Oh, right—none of your business." When he squinted into the shadows behind her, she added a sweet, "On both counts, Paul."

"Kind of makes this conversation pointless, doesn't it?" Reaching down the gullet of a mostly plucked turkey, he drew out a bloody liver. The grin he shot her resembled the Grinch's leer. "Hope you're not squeamish, Angel-eyes." He flipped the bird around, suspended it for her. "This big guy was up and running thirty minutes ago."

She merely smiled back. "Nice try, Paul, but I grew up in Alaska. I never did believe in the turkey tree. I did, however, read your latest column. Who's your source? And before you give me the standard reply, think Brian Pinkney in a bad mood, and my boss, who's under federal pressure to bring this killer in."

The reporter held up and balanced a long knife in his palm. "Even if I could answer your question, Angel, you know I wouldn't. Truth is, though," he tossed the knife in the air, caught it and squeezed the handle, "I haven't got a clue. Info just comes to me." The volume went up a notch. "Kind of like it does to you, Graydon." He cast a sly look into the dark. "It is you out there, isn't it? The great Noah Graydon. Seen by none, heard by only a select few. I'll cut you a deal. Let me see you, and I'll let you listen to my next message."

"Oh, good." Angel kept her own smile in place.

"That'll be phone taps for you, first thing tomorrow. Home, office and cell. We'll do your BlackBerry, too, and, of course, your computers. We're talking easy warrants here, Paul, because very few people even know about our John Doe, and while those who do almost certainly have their own opinions about his death, so far we haven't established a firm link between him and the Penny Killer. You, on the other hand, seem to have made the leap, so much so that you set your beliefs down in black and white and sent them out for everyone in the city to see. FBI doesn't like it when reporters do that. It hinders our investigation, and oh, just generally pisses us off. You want to save yourself a lot of grief, not to mention a thorough interrogation by people a lot less friendly than me. You really should think about cooperating."

He sucked on his mustache, regarded her through unreadable blue eyes. "You don't scare me, Angel. And it wouldn't matter if you did cut me off. He'd only go to someone else."

"Paul…"

"He's right." When Noah spoke, the reporter immediately strained for a better of view. But Angel knew exactly where he was, leaning casually against a tree trunk in his jeans, boots and signature black jacket.

Beneath Paul's cocky attitude, she sensed a measure of awe. Or maybe he simply recognized journalistic booty when he saw it.

"If you don't already know it, pal, you're on the verge of becoming a legend." Tossing the knife aside, the reporter hung his dead turkey on a pegged stand. "Trust me, I'm in the journalistic loop."

"Uh-huh." Noah sounded amused. "Not buying it, Reuben. You want the big story, and the book you figure will springboard from it. You won't get your wish, but you'll cling to the hope. Until your highly unstable source decides he's told you too much."

Paul's mouth turned down. "You don't know me, Graydon, or the killer. This is all bluster and speculation on your part."

Angel heard the shrug in Noah's voice. "I know you've got a pair of ex-wives and five kids under the age of ten to support. You live in a trailer and can only hook up to Brogan's water and electric when he figures you've done enough work to warrant the output. You pay child support, but resent it, hate your exes and your life, and you'd tell Angel pretty much anything she wanted to hear if you thought you stood a chance in hell of having sex with her."

Angel's eyes widened slightly, but she said nothing.

Noah continued in the same genial tone. "Hope's thinning for you, isn't it, Reuben, because deep in your gut, you're scared as hell of this guy. But you bought in, so what can you do except print what he tells you, then buy a bottle of whiskey and try to convince yourself that when the whole thing blows you'll be thrown clear, and maybe, finally, get to work on that never-gonna-happen book?"

Paul's face had gone from dull red to an odd shade of gray. Angel took that to mean Noah was dead on with his comments.

"So, Paul." Tapping his knee, she offered him an artless smile. "Are you ready to cooperate now?"

"I HAVE TO SAY I'M impressed." Angel welcomed the cold sting of wind on her face. "Grossed out, but amazed at your ability to read people."

"Reuben was easy. He started drooling the moment he saw you."

She slashed her hand sideways. "Way more than I need to know. I feel icky enough just having talked to him." She took note of the gravel parking lot they were walking through, with her one step ahead of him. "On the subject of icky, are you sure about this place? It looks a bit Slaughtered Lamb to me."

He kept her going with a hand pressed to the small of her back. "I said I'd buy you a drink, not sacrifice you to a moorland werewolf."

"Better an encounter with Lon than Bela. The count's never been my favorite creature of the night. But going back to Paul, I think he was drooling more over you than me. In a non-sexual way, of course." She did an air tracing of the burned out letters in front of her. "You know, with the *O* and the *U* not lit, your Roadhouse becomes a Radhose."

Noah's chuckle murmured through her blood-stream like fire-warmed brandy, a glass of which she suddenly wanted very badly. Closing her eyes, she visualized his face. Gorgeous, gorgeous, gorgeous, eye patch and all, so much so that she might have walked into the door if he hadn't reached around her to open it. Not cool, she re-flected, and, bumping a hand on the jamb, sent him a vaguely regretful look. "You're really messing me up, Graydon."

He caught her chin, pressed his thumb to her lower lip. "I understand messed up, Angel. Some days I swear I invented the term." His smile made her heart give a hard double thump. "After you."

She had to force concentration. "Reuben, news-paper article, suspect."

"Possible suspect," Noah corrected. "Also possible he's just a rat reporter who got lucky. He ran us in circles for the better part of that conversa-tion."

"It's his strong suit. I wonder if he's ever con-sidered going into politics."

"There's still time—if the killer doesn't turn on him."

"A prospect which, thanks to you, will weigh heavily on his mind for the next few days."

From the entry, Noah indicated a booth in the corner of what could at best be called an off-road dive. Angel counted over twenty men and a mere handful of women—all of whom were dressed in thigh-squeezing pants and barely there tops.

She smiled over her shoulder. "Such a sweetheart. You're trying to make me feel at home, aren't you? Because no less than ten of the men who are scowling at us look just like my dear old daddy."

"We can leave if you want to."

But she caught his jacket and held. "I'm teasing, Noah. Places like this don't affect me one way or the other. However, I can't resist the obvious question. Do you come here often?"

"Me, no. Graeme, yes."

She turned, stared. "Are you serious?" Stunned, she took in the seedy tables, damaged bar top and floors that felt like they were coated with a mixture of beer and chewing gum. "Why?"

"That's what Joe wants to know, or would if he realized his brother had been in here three nights out of the last four."

"Really." She digested that. "Wow. You know I haven't got a clue what to say, except I think we should be worried."

"Joe's been worried for days."

Brushing crumbs from the split vinyl seat, Angel slid into the booth. "Liz can't know about this, or she'd have told me."

"I think Liz has other things going on right now. You for one."

"You're chock full of charm tonight, aren't

you?" Shedding her coat, Angel set it aside. "First you bring me to a hole-in-the-wall bar, then you take me on a guilt trip… And if I'm only one thing, what's the other?"

"Let's do Reuben first, okay?"

"The rat reporter whose tipster might very well be our Penny Killer. Unless Paul cooperates— unlikely—and assuming he's not the killer himself—which is a fairly big assumption considering how well he handles a knife—whoever's behind the murders is bound to realize that we'll be all over him. How could we not be after that column he wrote? He all but stapled Foret and John Doe together, something we didn't even do until you—or rather I—put the word out this morning. Begs several more obvious questions and details I want to hear. However, for the moment I'll settle for wondering why we're having so much trouble identifying Mr. Doe. Brian thought he'd nailed it this afternoon, but like its predecessors, the DNA sample he shot to the lab said no."

"Sammy Reo?"

"You heard the buzz, huh? Brian insists the face is a match. Unfortunately, the computer and our lab techs beg to differ."

A sloe-eyed server with greasy hair delivered two glasses of beer they hadn't ordered and sashayed off to deliver more.

"You're sure this is where Graeme's been coming?" Angel rapped a knuckle on the splintered tabletop. "Here, where no one in his right mind has gone before or would go again on a dare?"

"One subject at a time, Angel." Noah drank, sat back.

She watched the server rearrange her breasts in a too-small bra, then set an elbow on the table and smiled into the hazel eye she could just about see. "Let's do a deal. We'll pick a topic and stay on it until it's exhausted. My choice, yeah?"

Humor came through in his easy, "Should I trust this deal?"

"Probably not, but I'll preface my selection by saying there's very little question that Paul Reuben knows far more than he's telling us, and that's definitely cause for concern. On a personal level, Graeme coming undone is even more disturbing to me. As far as John Doe's uncanny resemblance to a Manhattan drug lord is concerned, that particular riddle should be solvable within the next twelve hours. I'm thinking brother or possibly cousin, not on file with us or the police."

A dark brow shot up. "Which leaves?"

She eased closer, wouldn't let him look away. "I've been immersed in this investigation since 7:00 a.m., and it's well after 6:00 p.m. now. I want a break. I want to hear your John Doe theory and why you're convinced he's one of the Penny Killer's victims. I want you to talk to me. More than any of those things, though, I want you to kiss me. Right here." Catching the front of his jacket, she dragged him forward until her lips grazed his and she added a hungry, "Right now."

THE DAY DISSOLVED. So did most of the night. Angel could have devoured him—a sensation that was so out of character for her she barely recognized it.

Delicious, dark thoughts tumbled through her head. Desire stirred them together. She wanted Noah to the point where she was willing to put a murder investigation on hold in order to kiss him. That couldn't be right, could it?

"Five minutes," she said under her breath and had his lips twitching on hers.

"Gonna take a lot longer than that, Angel."

What she'd started, he deepened, holding her in place until every thought in her head puddled.

He used his tongue to discover her mouth, used his hands to excite her skin, taking the heat beneath the surface from a sizzle to a burn.

His mouth was open and equally hungry on hers. He cupped her face with his fingers, kissed her in a way that sent alternating jolts of astonishment and delight straight to her nerve ends.

Time and place… The words whispered at her. She didn't want him to stop for any reason, but as she pulled away to fill her lungs with much-needed air, it occurred to her that of all the times and places she could have chosen, this was un-doubtedly one of the worst.

Oh, but he was pure fascination, and when she touched him, every part of her, mind and body, shifted into sensory overdrive. Colors bled, sights and sounds receded. There was only the scent of his skin and hair, the taste of his mouth—uniquely Noah—and the fire that had already became an ache deep within her body.

For a moment, he rested his forehead against hers, stroked his thumb over her jaw, while his fingers tangled in her hair.

"I never thought a kiss could pack such a punch," she murmured. "I'm losing myself in you, Noah, and I don't think that's all good right now." However, as her balance returned, and with it a glimmer of playfulness, she added a teasing, "Of course, one has to wonder who'd want to be good all the time."

"It's never been my problem," he admitted, then grimaced slightly. "Uh, you might want to move your hand, Angel, before I show you just how not good I can be."

She glanced down. "Oops." Far from chastened, however, she let her fingers trail a sinuous path from the front of his jeans to the side of his neck, which she kissed and lightly nipped. "My choice of moments could be better, but I like what I'm feeling inside." She played with the ends of his hair. "Tell me, is everyone in the bar staring, or am I just hot and bothered because of you?"

A slow smile appeared—only to vanish a

second later. Swearing, he drew her with him into the shadows.

Angel knew better than to resist, however, she did risk a look to the side. "What's… Oh, hell."

The last two words sighed out as Graeme Thomas stumbled into the bar, gave the sloe-eyed server a kiss, then collapsed into a boneless heap on the floor.

Chapter Nine

They left Graeme's car, a Mercedes with a crushed fender on the driver's side, behind the bar. Angel drove him home in her CRV. Noah followed in his truck. They used the keys from his coat to access both the lobby and elevator and somehow managed to get him upstairs with only three people noticing.

"Think that was Aaron Milford," Graeme slurred, his arm draped heavily across Angel's shoulder. "I tell him to lose weight, but he owns bakeries and likes to sample. Ah." His face lit up. "Another dough boy. Different dough than yours... Why's that guy in black following us, Angel face?"

She winced when he stepped on her foot. "No guy, Graeme, only a product of your imagination."

"I don't imagine men."

"Then he must be a product of my imagination."

"Figment," he corrected with exaggerated clarity. His head swayed. "Not your type whoever he is. Hey, wait a minute. We should be at the hospital. I got stuff to do."

"Don't think so. What's your alarm code?" While she propped him against the wall, Noah pressed the buttons he rattled off on his seventh floor door.

Hooking his forearms over her shoulders, Graeme set his face close to hers. "Got some problems happening here, Angel."

"Yes, I sensed that."

He started to fall on her. With the door open, Noah took him by the arms. "I'll get him inside, Angel. You get the lights."

"Who are you?" Graeme demanded. "No bikers allowed in the building."

"Might want to mention that to Mr. Milford." Angel depressed the light switch. "I saw a Harley fob on his key ring... My God, Graeme, it looks like a bomb went off in here."

"Problems," he sang out from behind. "Tell your figment not to be so rough. Don't damage the hands. Hey, whoa, wait." His head lolled sideways to stare. "Are you Graydon?"

"No comment," Noah murmured. "Where do you want him?"

Angel swiped dirty laundry from a museum-quality chair. "Here's good. This is so weird, Noah. He was fine the last time I saw him."

"Which was?"

"Not sure. We missed each other at his niece's birthday party, so it must have been in the path lab when I was looking at Foret."

"Yuck face." Graeme grinned at Noah. "That's the expression she gets when she views corpses."

"Victims." On her knees beside the chair, Angel fought his trench coat off. "People who shouldn't be dead but are. Biggest yuck I can think of."

Graeme made a half turn to stare at her. "Are you undressing me?"

"I'm trying to."

"Is your figment going to stay and watch?"

"Not helping me here, Dr. T." She looked up at Noah. "Should one of us be calling Joe?"

Noah gave his head a faint shake, walked to the window.

"What then? Are we just going to leave him and hope he doesn't wander out? Graeme, lift your arm," she said with patience.

"Gonna build a bridge," he told her. "Gonna cross it and hide." His head hit Angel's with a thud. "Ouch." He rubbed it. "Did you know Liz keeps a journal? Don't think Joe knows, but I saw it."

Angel gave his coat a final firm tug. "Lots of people keep journals…" Suspicion snuck in, and she set a finger under his chin. "Graeme, did you read Liz's journal?"

"Oh, yeah. Better than Hansel and Gretel. Think that's the story I was telling Jaynie. Casserole's dinging. She sets the thing on Jaynie's dresser. Uh-oh, I've seen it now. I turn into Curious George. Aw damn, the book's got a lock. Kid's hairpin might do the trick. Bad Graeme, way too nosy, but hey, she's my sister-in-law. No secrets, right? Or, hmm, maybe there are." He made air quotes. "'Noah Graydon says there'll be a note.' Hmm again. 'Note will connect dead body—Lionel Foret's—to killer from the past. Note delivered before Foret died…' Not a nice entry, Liz. Not a nice thought." Reaching out, Graeme caught hold of Angel's hair. "If I build a big bridge, will you cross it with me and make the nightmare go away?"

Angel gave him a light shake when his forehead landed on her shoulder. "Come on, Graeme, don't pass out on me. What nightmare? Why do you want to build a bridge?"

Noah returned, went to his haunches behind her. As Graeme's body went limp, she exhaled her frustration and settled him as comfortably as possible in the chair.

"'Suffering is the bridge to understanding', Noah. That's what Foret's note said. Liz must have written about it in her journal. Now, suddenly Graeme wants to build a bridge to escape from a nightmare." She rocked her head to ease the tension in her muscles. "I hope you like puzzles because I'm too tired to make sense of a knock-knock joke at this point."

"What's in his pocket?"

Pushing on a nerve in her neck, Angel refocused. "Uh, that would be his hand."

He shot her a dry look.

She sighed. "You do understand tired, right?"

But even as she asked, she worked Graeme's hand out of his pants. "Looks like a wrinkled handkerchief, lovely, and a crumpled napkin."

"Which he's got squeezed in his fist."

"Yes, well have you seen his kitchen…?" She broke off, met Noah's stoical gaze.

"You or me?" he asked.

"I'll do it." She had to rub Graeme's wrist to unlock his rigid fingers. When she smoothed the napkin he'd been clutching, the stenciled letters jumped out as if they'd been scribed in blood.

YET ANOTHER BRIDGE IS BUILT.

BROTHER OF MAN SHALL SUFFER.

BUT WILL HE UNDERSTAND?

"WHY WOULD SOMEONE want to kill my brother?" Strands of Joe's hair stood up in spikes as he strode back and forth across Graeme's living room floor. "It's wrong, it's all wrong. Like this place." He swept a hand around the untidy room. "And him. You know he talks a good game, Angel, and God knows he likes women, but Graeme's a surgeon. That's the top of the medical totem pole. He never drinks to excess, and the women he dates enjoy him as much as he enjoys them. He simply doesn't have or make enemies. You need to do something, Noah."

"Speed seems to be important this time around," Noah remarked from the window ledge. "I'm not sure it was before."

"Great." Joe gave a croaky laugh. "Guy takes a five-year break, then accelerates the pace. Why didn't Graeme tell me about the note?"

"We don't know when he got it," Angel reminded him. "We can only assume he figured out its significance after he read Liz's journal entry."

"Journal entry." Joe rubbed a hand over his face. "Did I even know she kept a journal? No. Am I her husband or a complete stranger to the woman I married?" He appealed to Angel. "Why isn't she here?"

"I left a voice mail," Angel began, but Joe cut her off with another rusty bark of laughter.

"Voice mail and notes—it's how we communicate these days. Do you think Peloni has that trouble?"

Angel stopped tidying Graeme's end table. "What does Pete have to do…?"

Passing her, Noah murmured a quiet, "Later, okay?" Louder he said, "You need to suck it up, Joe. If not for your own sake, then for Graeme's."

"I know." He inhaled deeply, exhaled with a calming whoosh. "I know. Can and will do. Sorry, Angel, I didn't mean to have a panic attack. I'm out of practice with stuff like this. I used to get Graeme out of a lot of tough spots in high school and college. He didn't make enemies as such, but girls liked him, and sometimes guys resented that." He spread his hands. "What did the killer mean when he wrote 'Brother of man shall suffer'? Are we talking me specifically or the general brotherhood of man?"

Noah returned briefly to the window. "My opinion? Go with the brotherhood."

"Your opinion, but what if you're wrong? And what's to understand beyond the fact that the guy who's doing this is a frigging homicidal maniac—and I emphasize the word 'maniac'."

Angel wished she could think of something to say that would comfort him, but short of mentioning that she'd received a note very similar to Graeme's, there wasn't much. She was also curious about his reference to Pete Peloni and Liz and what that might or might not entail.

Sprawled in his chair, an oblivious Graeme snored, with his mouth open and his normally well-groomed hair hanging over his forehead.

"Dr. McDreamboat," she said, and earned a stare from the other two men. "That's what the female hospital staff members call him." She fingered Graeme's hair. "Guess they watch *Grey's Anatomy*. Which brings me back to Joe's point that Graeme's a 'make friends' kind of guy, not the sort of person anyone would want to murder."

Noah started going through the kitchen cupboards. "Could be one of his transplant ops didn't take, and someone in the family blames him for it."

"Would that same person blame Foret for a different screw-up, and that cop five or six years ago for something else? And what about the soccer mom and the marketing director and the CEO…?"

"Yeah, I know, Angel. I get it." He closed the drawer he'd been rifling through and came back into the living room. "My point is that all options have to be kept open, even the most unlikely ones."

"Which brings us to the least-likely-suspect-could-very-well-be-our-killer scenario."

"Lot of people on that list," Joe remarked. Following Noah's lead, he opened some cabinet doors. "You, Noah, Bergman… Liz."

Angel didn't miss the slight hesitation. Dipping into her coat pocket, she pressed the redial for her partner's cell. And was directed once again to voice mail. "Back in a minute," she said, and arranging Graeme's head into a more comfortable position, started for the bathroom.

Boosting herself onto the granite counter, she punched a different number.

"Good evening, Peloni's."

She wouldn't think the worst, wouldn't, no matter what Joe implied. "Hi, Pete, it's Angel. Is Liz there?"

"Uh…well…uh."

Oh God. "Put her on, okay?"

"I'm not sure…"

"FBI stuff happening here, Pete. Put her on."

She listened to Madonna until a defensive sounding Liz came on the line. "Who told you I was here?"

"You don't want to know. I'm at Graeme's condo with Noah and Joe. He has a note."

"Who has a note?" A quaver crept in. "Joe?"

"Graeme. He got a note like mine and Foret's, and he knows it's a threat because he read your journal, which, locked or not, you should never leave in plain sight on a kid's dresser." Unable to stop herself, she lowered her voice to demand, "Liz, is Pete your great-aunt Trudy?"

"What? Of course not. You know my aunt. You met her in Taunton last spring, at my cousin Minnie's wedding."

"I remember. She was wearing a rose garden on her body and her head. But did she really burn two Cornish hens to a crisp last week?"

"Angel, please. I need you to take me on faith with this."

Angel's heart sank. "There's a this?"

"There's always a this in my life. There's been a this of some sort since I was five and my kid brother lit our neighbor's garage on fire because he refused to believe that any form of liquid could burn. Guess what? Whiskey burns. Please do this for me."

"I don't want to lie to Joe."

"I'm not asking you to lie. Well, maybe a little. Does he know you're talking to me right now, or did you duck into the bathroom?"

Liz knew her way too well, Angel realized. On the flip side, did she know anything at all about her partner?

Rubbing her temple, she whispered a soft, "That's a really depressing question."

"It is?"

"Talking to myself here, Liz, not you. Yes, all right. I won't say anything to Joe."

"Or Noah."

"It's a miracle I don't get migraines. Okay, or Noah. But at some point, you have to explain, agreed?"

"Agreed." Relief oozed through Liz's voice. "I'm on my way. Twenty minutes. Tell Joe—well, be clever. Say Minnie's having a marital crisis and I had to play referee."

"Think I'll stick with your great-aunt Trudy." As she hopped from the counter, Angel made the mistake of glancing into the sink. "Whiskers. Lovely." She dusted off the back of her coat. "Do you want to know what the note said…? Liz?" When her partner didn't respond, she pressed end and slipped the cell back in her pocket. "Weirder and weirder."

She flushed for good measure, washed her hands and while she was at it de-whiskered the sink. She didn't blame Graeme for being rattled to the point of strange behavior. What she didn't understand was, after reading Liz's journal, why he hadn't come forward with his note?

Although the subtle bathroom light generally flattered, Angel avoided the mirror and instead dug a bottle of non-prescription painkillers from the medicine cabinet. Bolstered, she blew out a short breath, opened the door. And crashed right into Noah's chest.

Had he heard her talking to Liz? It was her first thought, and she prayed it didn't show. "Sorry." She extended her hand, palm up. "Needed aspirins."

"Yeah?" Sliding a knuckle under her chin, he tipped her head back. "I see more turmoil than pain in those beautiful eyes, Angel."

In which case, he saw entirely too much.

"How's Graeme?"

He let it go with a barely perceptible curve of his lips. "Better than Joe."

Okay, maybe he wasn't so much letting it go as letting her know she could talk to him. But she'd known that since their first conversation eighteen months ago.

Disinclined to make excuses, she sidestepped and started down the hall. But five steps on, she turned. "It's never simple, is it? Life, I mean. It's all bumps and curves and things you don't expect. Couldn't expect because they blindside you."

"Let it go for tonight, Angel. The worst things often look better after a period of separation."

A laugh slipped out. "Cryptic notes, cryptic statements. I get the concept, Noah. I'm just not sure it works for me."

"She told you not to say anything, didn't she?"

Angel walked back to him. "No way could you

have heard that conversation. So either you've got some kind of interceptor implanted in your head, or Graeme's bathroom's bugged, in which case I'm quitting this job right now."

The faint smile lingered. "I saw you leave with your cell phone. I saw the look on your face. I also saw Liz."

Confusion moved in. "When? Tonight?"

"A few nights ago, outside your place. While Pete was delivering the food he promised you, Liz was waiting in his truck."

She stared. "While *Pete* was delivering... You know him?"

"Not the point."

"It is to me. How?"

"Dog with a bone," he murmured.

"Cat with a fish, says Joe. Speaking of whom, does he know Liz was with Pete...? Wait a minute." The significance suddenly struck her. "Liz was with Pete? In his truck?" Gripping his jacket, Angel let her head drop onto Noah's shoulder. "My God, what's going on in this nightmare? Why doesn't any of it make sense? Seemingly nice people are dead, people from the past and the present. I've been threatened, Graeme's been threatened, we have a murdered corporate lawyer and a John Doe. Paul Reuben's probably been consorting with a killer, and Liz has been consorting with Pete Peloni in his truck. Joe's suspicious, I'm worried, and all we seem to have are a lot of square pegs that refuse to fit into our round holes."

She felt his hand stroking her hair and couldn't deny she liked it. Score one for an otherwise freakish night.

"We'll modify the holes, Angel, and in time those pegs will fit."

"I don't want to spy on Liz," she said into his shoulder.

"Neither do I. So we'll do it the other way."

"Spy on Pete?" Raising her head, she met his shadowed gaze. "That's not a whole lot more appealing."

"More practical, though." Noah held her stare. "I ran a computer check on the guy as a favor to Joe. He bought Peloni's two years ago. Before that he worked in the meat industry in Texas."

She knew what was coming. Didn't want to hear it but knew all the same. "I'm going to need more than two pills, aren't I?"

"Depends on how you look at it. Before he became a restaurateur, Peter Levon Peloni was a butcher."

THE FRUSTRATION LEVEL HAD reached new heights. The message simply wasn't getting through. Something more straightforward was needed, must be needed if even Noah Graydon couldn't figure it out.

Strategic maneuvering might work. Steer them to the ugly truth. Make them look and see and deal.

Make the truly guilty parties pay.

Chapter Ten

"Got it…I hope."

Cautiously optimistic after days of nothing on nothing, Angel went over the feed from Florida twice before she e-mailed Noah.

"We have an ID on John Doe," she typed. "His name's Luki Romero, and guess what? He's Sammi Reo's brother. Possibly good, possibly bad, but never charged, never even arrested. We have no pictures, prints or DNA and no history because, well, if he is a baddie, he's never been caught, unlike his big brother who's pitching a fit in Miami as we speak. Apparently Sammi's been in South America for the past ten days. Hmm… Anyway, Mr. No-Can-Touch Reo's given us a photo ID, which gives our latest victim a name, if little else. Call me ASAP. Liz and I are going to the hospital to talk to Graeme. I sense a high-stress day in the works."

She heard the whir of Brian's wheelchair, swung

to greet him—and wound up laughing at his squished-up expression.

"Have you ever tried for a not-grumpy Papa Bear look, Bri?"

He balled his fists. "I'm coming with you."

"Wha-at?" Laughter continued to tickle her throat. She couldn't have heard him right. "To the hospital?"

"If that's where you're going, that's where I'm coming. Your partner is unavailable this afternoon."

As she had been all morning and probably wished she'd remained last night.

The scene at Graeme's had been tense to say the least, the strain between Liz and Joe a tangible thing. For someone who hated secrets, Liz was sticking stubbornly by the one between her and Pete. Stick any harder, Angel reflected, and her marriage would go from a little frayed to completely unbound.

Not her business, really, but with two friends involved and having been dragged in on the periphery, both guilt and concern weighed heavily on her mind.

To Brian, she said, "Have you read Graeme's note?"

"Read it, puzzled over it, waiting now for Graydon—oh, sorry, I mean you—to wow us with your thoughts on it. I'm also waiting for an explanation of his—your John Doe-is-one-of-the-Penny-Killer's-victims statement."

"Luki Romero." Unperturbed, Angel swiveled her monitor. "Our John Doe is the unknown brother of well-known drug lord Sammi Reo."

Brian's mouth opened as he squinted at the screen. "Huh. Good stuff. I'm surprised anyone was able to nail Reo down long enough to make him listen. Guy's like smoke most of the time. You think you can nab him, but make the attempt and he's gone in a puff."

"No pun intended, right?" Angel checked her gun, dropped her badge inside her long, gunmetal gray coat and gave her desk a quick scan. "I assume you've seen Paul Reuben's column on Foret and Doe, aka Romero?"

"Read it front to back three times. Bergman's cleared me to have a chat with the guy." He cast her a look of dubious gratitude. "Guess I can thank you for that bone."

She grinned. "You're welcome. Now let's get to Graeme before he figures out we're coming and bolts."

"Why would a guy under threat of death bolt? Where would he bolt to?"

"Don't know, twice. But something's up with him, and I want to know what it is."

"Before he gets his eyes gouged out?"

"If that's the killer's new MO, yes. Definitely before the pennies appear. Can you walk?"

Brian whirred ahead of her to the elevator. "Well enough to work outside this dull hole for a few hours." He punched the call button with a vengeance and a tick in his jaw that told Angel something more hostile than usual was brewing below the surface.

"Wanna share?" she asked while they waited.

He looked at her, ticked faster. "I like you, Angel."

When he didn't continue, she swept uncertain eyes from side to side. "Okay, I'm glad. Is there an 'and' or a 'but'?"

"You're going to get hurt. You could get killed. Will get killed if you work too closely with Noah Graydon. He's—dangerous."

Angel stared in astonishment. Where had that come from? "Uh, Brian, Noah's one of the good guys, remember? He creates criminal profiles, and does it very well."

"So say you. I say he's had two shots at the Penny Killer and where's that so-called expertise of his gotten us? Seven deaths, a five-year break, two new victims and a third under threat."

"Brian, Noah's not…"

He cut her off with a steely look. "Don't, just don't. Pruneface Skater's nothing more than a figurehead Bergman tossed in to placate Graydon's boss. Fine, whatever. But we know the truth, you and me and anyone else with half a brain. Your favorite phantom's poking along like a snail on crutches. Pruneface's turtle mode could keep pace easily, then and now."

Her patience intact but straining, Angel swung on her heel to face him. "Noah was a field agent five years ago, Brian. Maybe he did some profiling on his own dime, but it wasn't his job. You're judging him on a past that isn't valid. On top of which, a profile is only a profile. In the end, it's down to us to figure out who the murderer is and make the arrest. With evidence."

"Like a pair of gouged-out eyeballs?"

When the elevator opened, Angel barred Brian's entry with a palm pressed against the door. "The victim's eyes weren't gouged out, they were simply gouged, in the same way that he was stabbed through the heart after death. We suspect a copycat, but Noah says nada. Why? Not sure yet, but you can bet your life if Bergman's on board it's a valid no."

Brian stuck his chin out. "Then why doesn't Graydon…?"

"Elaborate? Details, Brian. They have to be in order before he can lay it out and say yes, we're definitely looking at another Penny Killer victim. You've heard the cliché about closing doors and opening windows. You worked in the field, you know how it has to be. Until Noah has the information required, all doors remain open. We're clear on that, yeah?"

She used her foot to hold the elevator so she could set her hands on Brian's wheelchair. "I know you dislike Noah. Maybe for personal reasons, maybe because you worked together on his first gig in Boston. But like him or not, he's the best profiler in the business, and for all your bluster, I don't believe you'd be any farther along with this case than he is. If," she added with emphasis "he was actually on this case. Unless of course there's something you know that you're not telling." Her brows rose. "Is there something, Brian, or are you just being an ass because the vehicle accident that injured your spine occurred while you were en route to a warehouse where a certain young FBI agent was trying to prove his mettle to a talented superior? A young agent you stumped for strongly on recruitment."

Brian seethed so hard Angel was surprised steam didn't shoot from his ears. "The kid had potential, and Graydon screwed up. End result, the kid died. The Penny Killer got him. And Graydon walked away."

"Don't think so, Bri." But she softened her tone when she glimpsed the sorrow that came and went, lightning quick from his eyes. "Noah's file might be classified beyond my ability to access it, but I'm guessing it didn't go down quite as simply as that. Now you can either tell me how it really was, or stonewall me and let the truth come out another way. It's your choice. But one thing's for sure. We're going to the hospital, and we're talking to Graeme. Because he's alive. And I'm going to do everything I can to make sure he stays in that condition." Straightening, she fixed a smile on her lips and released the door. "Coming?"

COFFEE, AS THICK AS INK and about that drinkable, kept Noah going through another long night in his truck. He watched Angel's window and worked his computer to within an inch of its state-of-the-art life.

By 6:00 a.m., he had facts, figures, documents and photos piled up on the seat beside him. He also had a slamming headache and the very strong urge to hit something. Hard.

A gym would do, or a certain restaurant owner. Paul Reuben in a pinch, although that guy had enough of his own problems to deal with.

When Angel drove out of the condo parking lot, he headed home for a hot shower and a change of clothes.

There were messages from Joe everywhere, on his voice and e-mail, his BlackBerry and his PC.

Liz refused to talk about anything that mattered. All Joe had managed to get out of her was a comment about last night being the first time she'd seen Noah. Not that she had gotten a clear look at him—there'd been plenty of long shadows in Graeme's loft—but her impression had been that he was younger than she'd expected. Younger, fitter and darker.

Angel had done everything in her power to keep the situation on level ground. Not her fault it had sloped downward. And crash-landed in the end.

Ignoring the rest of his messages, Noah postponed his workout in favor of another marathon computer session. By three o'clock, however, he'd had enough. He needed air and that punching bag badly. What he didn't need was to see the car parked behind his truck as he exited the back of the building.

Swollen storm clouds hung overhead. The alley was narrow and murky by nature. He only had to select a spot between truck and wall to remain a silhouette—which he did with an attitude of mild mistrust as the car's driver approached.

"I've been waiting for you," Liz Thomas said quietly. "Joe doesn't know I'm here. Neither does Angel. I need a favor."

She needed a great deal more than that. "Does it concern Joe?"

She attempted to penetrate the veil of darkness surrounding him. "It's—no. You're friends. I'm not looking to drive any wedges. What I want is for you to watch Angel, because I can't right now. There are things going on that keep pulling me sideways."

Or pulling her apart, Noah reflected. He ran his gaze over her drawn face. "Is there some reason you can't talk to Angel about those things?"

She gave a tremulous breath of laughter. "Well, yeah. Like the fact that she has a death threat hanging over her head and flatly refuses to tell Bergman about it. She's chasing a killer who's chasing her. And now he's chasing Graeme as well.

I've got kids who want attention, a marriage that needs attention, a partner in trouble and a brother-in-law, also in trouble, who's decided that getting drunk will make the killer go away. I'm good with pressure, but not the best with uber stress, especially on a personal level. And like I told Angel, I think secrets suck."

"They do."

"Will you do it, Noah? Will you watch her and not stop watching her until this lunatic with the knife is either dead himself or behind bars for life?" One shoulder twitched, then the other. "Because I don't want her to die and know I might have been able to stop it from happening if I'd been sharper or faster, or just there in the first place like I should be right now."

Noah looked up and away, pictured—a lot of things, really. Angel for the most part, but a killer behind her and a warehouse. And the face of a young agent who should be tracking criminals instead of rotting in a pine box in a Washington cemetery.

"I am watching her, Liz." He brought his gaze back. "That's not going to change."

She worried her bottom lip. "Who is this guy, anyway? Are we talking about a split personality or a pissed-off sociopath? He's so specific with his MO in the majority of cases, and yet his victims are about as non-specific as you can get."

"They're specific," he told her. "I just haven't

gotten far enough into his head to determine what those specifications are."

"But how can you tie a soccer mom to Angel, and from there to Foret and Graeme?"

"I'm building a profile. The guy won't be disappearing for five years again." He regarded her through his lashes. "He also won't be getting Angel, no matter who he is—reporter, farmer or former Texas butcher."

IT WAS AFTER 9:00 P.M. when Angel finally got home.

"Ick, yuck, bleckh." Jumping from her CRV, she endeavored to shake the mental residue from her limbs. It didn't work. She'd need a scraper to remove the creepy sensations from her body. Being immersed in a hornets' nest would have been more appealing than what she'd gone through this afternoon. And for nothing but excuses and avoidance in the end. Never, ever again.

She spotted his truck as she was unlocking the front door. Perfect. She'd only called him for four hours straight, until her cell phone had died and Brian's with it. Now, here he was, and here she was— and why the hell hadn't he checked his voice mail?

He was out and waiting by the time she strode across the street. Grabbing his hair, she yanked him down, kissed him hard, then shoved.

"That I made it home as early as nine o'clock is no thanks to you or your message service, Graydon. Was your phone even turned on today?"

"I heard about the elevator, Angel."

"Did you also hear that I was stuck inside it with a dead body, two morgue attendants and Brian Pinkney for five hours that read more like five days? 'You don't mind riding with a covered corpse, do you, Angel?' one of the nurses asks me. 'The regular elevator banks are backed up. Guess we have an overload of visitors today.'

"Okay, no problem, I'll tough it out. Graeme's doing a consult—an extra-long one, I'm convinced, because no way does he want to face me after last night. Why? No idea, but Joe says he's being totally evasive about the hows, wheres and whens of that note we found in his pocket. Seems like a weird reaction to me, but I'm not about to interrupt a consultation for a heart transplant patient when I see the family holding hands and praying in the waiting room. Brian and I can have coffee, come back in an hour. Assuming we can get to the cafeteria. Ergo, the service elevator, morgue guys and one very dead body."

"Angel…"

"Not done yet, Graydon. We're not talking about your ordinary dead body here. This one had gangrene. I saw the guy's foot. Bad enough, you'd think, but then Brian saw it, and started to hyperventilate. Turns out he's a major hypochondriac, and a claustrophobic. So what do you think happened next?"

"The elevator broke down."

"Bingo. But we didn't know that right away, because first the power failed and service elevators aren't high priority in terms of the back-up generators." Bunching his jacket in her fists, she shook. "I was in there forever, Noah. I called you until my phone died. Why didn't you answer?"

He covered her hands with his. Despite her agitation, she noticed that he was still using the shadows to conceal himself. "I didn't get your messages," he told her. "My phone died a different kind of death this morning. I dropped it. I didn't know it wasn't working until I heard about the problems at the hospital from Bergman's assistant and tried to call you. By the time I got there, the problem was repaired and you were gone."

A chill rippled through her. "Brian went for a quick fix from the inside."

"You're joking."

Her lips tipped up. "Oh, no, dead serious. And speaking of dead, did you know he carries a knife? In a strap? On his ankle? It has a long, thin blade and folds up into itself. He says he used to hunt gophers when he was young, claims he's better with a knife than a gun. Today he used it to fiddle with the panel. Made both me and the attendants more than a little nervous when he went from twisting screws to stabbing them, but he insists that was sheer desperation."

"Was it?"

"Maybe. By then I just wanted out. Ah, but

nothing's that simple, is it? A few minutes after the screw-stabbing incident, he pulled a handkerchief from his pocket to wipe his face, and lo and behold, a bunch of pennies came out with it. Scattered all over the floor." She made a rainfall motion with her fingers. "Like rose petals. One landed on the dead man's sheet. I tell you, Noah, it's been a stellar day. I couldn't get Brian back to the office and his wheelchair fast enough. Now, all I can see is my once-trusted coworker with pennies in one hand, a knife in the other and a foot that's being eaten away by gangrene. It's gross, and I want it gone from my head." She breathed out twice, gave her arms a final shake and squared up. "Okay, now I'm done and taking my mother's advice from this moment on. She insists that tomorrow is open to all manner of possibilities, and ninety percent of them will be good. Means keep a positive attitude, which I try to do no matter what. Anyway, tomorrow has to be better than today, because today sucked."

"Your mom sounds like a cheerful woman."

"It's cheerfulness born of necessity. And twenty-five years of emotional hell later, I have to admit things worked out for her, so who am I to argue?"

"Do you ever talk about your father?"

"Noah, I don't even like to think about him. Memories creep in, I boot them out. Sounds like denial, but it isn't, not in the accepted sense. Sometimes Liz and I do Tai Chi. I let the past in then, deal with it in a controlled way and hope that eventually I'll get to a place where I'll be able to let it go completely. Like I'm going to let this elevator thing and my twisted picture of Brian go."

He grinned. "You planning to do some Tai Chi now?"

"Nope. Planning to take another deep breath, and ask with belated sincerity how your day went."

"It came a distant second to yours, I'm afraid." Still in the shadows, he brought her fingers to his lips and kissed them. "The biggest thing I did, other than work on the Penny Killer profile until my computer and my brain started blipping out, was dig into the life of one Pete Peloni."

Delighted by his action, Angel almost missed the second part. Until she heard Pete's name. "He's not—you know—" she made a implicative head motion "—with Liz, is he?"

"No, but not for the reason you'd think. Like that guy you spent the better part of your afternoon with, Peter L. Peloni, former butcher from a small Texas town, was discovered behind the cabin where he was born and raised. Pete Peloni's dead, Angel. He's been that way for the last three years."

Chapter Eleven

Angel could absorb a great deal, could separate, digest and compartmentalize with the best of them. But she couldn't accept that her best friend and partner might be aiding and abetting an identity thief. Noah had to be mistaken. If not that, then there was more than one Peter Levon Peloni in the country.

Levon though? It was hardly a common middle name.

Since neither of them had eaten dinner, they made the seven-mile trek to the Crystal Room. Food came second to the witchy atmosphere, but the fact that a certain victim-linked psychic reader named Phyllis was working there tonight made the choice a natural.

For the first time since Angel had seen him at Brogan's farm, Noah removed his jacket. No surprise to her, he had a great body, all sinew and lean, toned muscle, beautifully delineated beneath a dark blue T. Even the hair on his forearms was perfect. Yet for all that, she still didn't have a clear view of his face.

It was a thing Angel sensed she could push. She also knew she wouldn't. Not now.

When the coffee they'd ordered arrived, she leaned forward on her arms. "I won't let this take precedence over the Penny Killer investigation, Noah, but I can't get it out of my head. If Pete's not Pete, then who is he? Does Liz know?"

Noah took a pretzel from one of the crystal bowls. "What do you think?"

She gave a dark laugh. "I think I'd like to zap the discovery out of my life. Is there enough magic in this room to do that? No? Okay then, she knows. Which suggests a whole whack of possibilities I'm not prepared to deal with right now. How did you find out?"

"Don't you mean why was I looking?"

Desperate for a caffeine hit, Angel pried the lid off a canister decorated with moons and stars. "Sick of this day, yes, stupid, no. Obviously you did it for Joe. The how is more complex. If someone takes on another person's identity, he must feel fairly confident that he can do so safely, or why not invent a new one?"

"Because stealing's a ready-made solution."

"To what? Never mind. That's a question for Pete—or whoever he is." She dropped three cubes of sugar into her mug.

He spread his fingers. "All I did was backtrack

through Peloni's life. The route took me from here to a town call Yoke Bend, population seven, deep in the heart of southwest Texas.

"A few months ago, an old man from Yoke Bend moseyed into the county seat, said he had something he wanted someone in authority to see. He and a county cop went to Peloni's abandoned cabin, and there he was, or there his body was, wedged deep inside a dried up well."

"Murdered?"

"Not sure yet, but certainly dead for more than three years."

"What's the story?"

"My guess? He fell into the well and died. Our Pete found out about it, saw a golden opportunity and grabbed it. The real Pete was a rover, so if he took off all of a sudden, who of his seven fellow townspeople was going to mention it?"

"Maybe none, but didn't Pete One have an employer? You said he was a butcher by trade, right?"

"Off and on in Laredo. More off than on after his thirtieth birthday."

"Mid-life crisis come early?"

"It's as good a guess as any. By my estimation, he was thirty-six when he died."

"I gather he was unattached in the spousal as well as familial sense."

"Grandma Peloni passed away ten years ago. That was the extent of his family ties. There's no record of a wife or ex."

"So we're talking major loner here." She gave her coffee an absent stir. "I'm confused, Noah, and really not liking this, because not only does it make our Pete an identity thief, but it also means he knew the real Pete was dead and didn't report it. Unless Pete Two killed Pete One, which makes a certain amount of sense but scares the hell out of me for Liz's sake." She propped an elbow on the table, chin in hand. "So what do we do now? Hold or tell?"

"Hold for the moment, until we can get an ID on Pete Two. Shouldn't be difficult. All we'll need are prints."

"That's all we'll need if he has a record. Otherwise it'll be a little trickier."

"He'll have a record," Noah promised. "And it won't be pretty."

"I could talk to Liz," Angel said. "See if…" Trailing off, she stared at one of the papered black screens that divided the room into sections. "I think that's Lionel Foret's mother, Joy."

Noah followed her gaze. "Yeah, that's her."

The tease was automatic. "Maybe she's hoping to bring her son back to life through a psychic. You know, like the Monkey's Paw… No, stop right there, Angel." The tease faded to a headshake. "That was just plain mean. I'm usually more sensitive than that." With her eyes still on Joy, she halted the coffee mug halfway to Noah's mouth. "Not so fast, Graydon. I know we've talked about her, but just how is it you recognize Foret's mom?"

"She's a police dispatcher. Picture's on file. So's her history. She screwed up a major police bust last summer."

"Yes, I heard. I was hoping her captain would wipe it."

"He couldn't." Noah pushed his menu aside, rested a forearm on the table. Angel had to work at not being seriously distracted. "It was too extensive an op."

"We're talking about the setup of a guy who steals and strips vehicles, right?"

"That's part of what he does."

"And the rest?"

"Imports illegal weapons, perpetrates Internet fraud when he can, does a little illegal gambling when the mood strikes."

"A jack-of-all-trades. I wonder if Joy knew that."

"Whether she knew it or not, she blew the bust. Didn't mean to, which is why her captain defended her, but the end result was less than positive. A month after the aborted op, the guy murdered two teenagers who got in the way of an auto theft. They were making out in the boy's parents' Lamborghini."

Angel sighed. "You're not improving my day here, Noah. Please tell me this creep's not still walking around free."

"Cops got him cold for murder. But he should have been gone long before it reached that point."

Angel regarded the woman across the room.

"Poor parents. Poor kids." She couldn't help it. "Poor Joy, having to live with that. A guilty conscience, a dead son, two dead husbands and a boyfriend who likes tarantulas. That woman's got some very bad karma happening. I hope Paul Reuben doesn't hear about her blunder. He'll spin it into a headline-grabbing story that'll make *Mommy Dearest* read like *The Brady Bunch* by comparison."

Noah watched Joy gulp green tea as fast as it was poured. "Word is Reuben's been incommunicado ever since our chat at Brogan's farm."

"Score one for the hellish day." Returning her chin to her palm, Angel nodded at a woman with black-and-white hair, black lips and a long black dress that didn't quite cover her ample breasts. "That's Phyllis, yeah? Gonna do a reading for Joy? No wonder the poor thing's overdosing on tea. She has to be worried about what she'll hear."

"She'll hear what she wants to, Angel. Reuben did."

"The never-gonna-happen book deal?"

"If that was his biggest want. Phyllis gave Reuben the same reading she gives everyone. Different phrases, different emphasis, but the same spiel."

Angel's eyes sparkled. "Fess up, Graydon. You were the spoilsport at the birthday party who told the other kids how the rabbit really disappeared, weren't you?"

Humor glinted briefly. "Not quite. I'm the one who made it disappear to start with."

Disbelief stopped her laugh. "Seriously?"

"My father was an amateur magician. He taught me how to vanish rabbits, make playing cards spin in mid air and win the shell game every time."

Angel wished she could see his face. Regardless, she risked a soft, "And then?"

"He died. I was seventeen."

"Is your mother…?" She let the question hang.

But his body language made it clear he had no problem with that aspect of his past. "She died when I was twenty-five. I had good parents, Angel. No siblings and only a handful of other relatives, most of them in Queensland and unknown to me."

"Your parents were Australian?"

"My father was. My mother came from Donegal."

"The things you learn when you come to a psychic tearoom." As Phyllis left Joy and started toward their table, she tickled his wrist. "Thanks for that, Noah."

"You might want to hold off with those thanks until after you talk to Phyllis. The only way she'll answer questions is via a reading."

"Oh, good."

"She's already done me."

"Better still." Angel watched the psychic approach through her lashes. "I'll be fine," she said, "as long as she doesn't get me going on bats."

AN HOUR LATER, ANGEL had as many answers as Phyllis would give, and a reading that was almost as vague as the Penny Killer's notes.

"I'm a study in contrasts and contradictions," she told Noah after they'd exited the tearoom. "My life's in transition, both on a personal and a professional level. I'm emotionally conflicted, but that won't prevent me from achieving my goals."

Noah tried not to smile. "Which are?"

"To be successful in my career while striking a balance between that and my relationship. She foresees a family, but not for a few more years. When I asked her how many kids, she wouldn't say. What she would say, after a fair bit of prodding, is that Paul Reuben has a dark side to his nature that could be easily perverted. I took that to mean, if he hooks up with Obi-Wan, he might make it. Fall in with Darth Vader, and he's sunk…"

Noah opened the passenger door of his truck. "I liked Han Solo myself."

"Conflicted character." Angel kissed his right cheek. "Like nine-tenths of the human race. Totally identifiable." She studied his partly hidden features. "You have a purposeful look about you. Are we going somewhere?"

"To a club I know." He got in, slammed his own door and checked the computerized panel for messages.

"Weird vibe?"

"Off the scale."

"Good." She stared through the windshield at the traffic streaming left to right past the parking lot. "I'm sick of trying to make sense of things that might never have any sense attached to them."

"Such as?"

"Graeme's behavior." She scissored her hands. "No idea what's going on inside his head. If I got a note that I knew was a death threat, I'd go straight to the authorities."

"You got a note, Angel, and you refused to go to the authorities."

She struggled with the frustration that wanted to rise. "Your perversity's showing, Graydon. I *am* the authority on this case. Part of it anyway. Which brings me to Liz's behavior. She's been the steady one ever since I've known her. I go up, I go down, she stays level. What's happening now is like when a parent gets really old, and suddenly the child's in charge. It feels turned around. Joe's upset and angry, and who can blame him, Brian's carrying a fold-up knife in an ankle strap, Paul Reuben's vanished, and I swear, back at the Crystal Room, I saw Foret's mother pouring something from a flask into her tea."

"What makes you think that's unusual?"

"I don't. Point is, I thought about borrowing the flask." Hooking a leg beneath her, she regarded him in profile. Stunning but still shadowed. "Say something positive, Noah, something that'll make this night seem not so creepy."

"There's no one following us."

"Good so far."

"You're beautiful."

She grinned. "Even better." Then sighed. "I don't suppose, from a profiler's perspective, there's any chance the killer might decide he's had enough and just, you know, go away."

"Not in Kansas here, Dorothy."

"That's a no." She played with the buttons on her coat, would rather have played with the ends of his hair, but that would be pushing it. "I have this big question mark in my head, Noah. Why bridges and suffering and constant bids for understanding? If the killer wants us to understand, all he has to do is stop being so damned cryptic. You say he feels superior. Fine, but he needs to spell his message out for the lowly rest of us, because cryptic's just not cutting it. Ah…" Since she couldn't play with his hair, she wound a strand of her own around her finger. "That's where Paul Reuben comes in, isn't it? He's the human messenger."

"That'd be my guess. Message goes through Reuben to the FBI and beyond that to the world."

"Great, but it still doesn't decrypt the message. He wants us to build a metaphorical bridge linking suffering to understanding—Foret's note. Then the circle of understanding will be complete—my note. When will that completion occur? When I die?"

"You're not going to die, Angel."

She covered a quick spike of fear with a smile. "I love it when you talk tough. Moving on, another bridge is built. Brother of man suffers this time. But again, the question of understanding arises. Graeme's note. Put them together and you have two sufferings, two bridges, three understandings and one complete circle. You also have one man, Luki Romero, whose note we haven't located yet."

"Have you even located his home?"

"I talked to Liz from the elevator. Luki has an apartment in the Back Bay area, but it's more like a city broom closet than somewhere he'd have lived. His brother's no help. All he'll say is that Luki was born lucky. My translation—Luki was as corrupt as brother Sammi. He just managed never to get caught. According to Liz's best street sources, buzz is that Luki was a mastermind thief. Robbed from the rich, gave to himself. So it looks as though at least one of our victims was a baddie. Still doesn't explain Foret or the soccer mom or the cop, etc, etc, etc."

At a traffic light, Noah watched a group of college kids clowned their way through the crosswalk. "I sense a downward spiral this time. The killer's rushing toward a predetermined end that wasn't there before."

"Is it possible he's dying and wants to finish up before he goes?"

"Maybe. It feels more like he's losing or has lost part of his original focus. That could be driven either by impatience or frustration. We're not getting it. He's starting to resent that. From his perspective, it's crystal clear. Why can't we see?"

Unease churned like a noxious potion in Angel's stomach. "Do you think he'll come for me next, or Graeme?"

"Even under surveillance, if it boils down to opportunity, he'd have more of it with Graeme. On the other hand, you're the one he sees as completing the circle."

"The circle," she mused. "Brother of man. Noah, is it possible that Graeme's note was directed at Joe rather than him?"

"Why?"

She connected what few dots she had. "Well, Joe's done the pathology on a number of the Penny Killer's victims."

"Which means?"

"There might be a clue in his reports."

"Have you gone over those reports?"

"I'm running out of dots here, Graydon. Yes, I have, and no, I haven't seen anything out of the ordinary in them. Connection terminated."

"Temporarily aborted. I never terminate, Angel, only stick things in a slot based on degree of probability."

She smiled. "I love dirty talk, too. Are we almost at this club of yours?"

"Not mine." He made a right onto a street lined with smoky blue signs.

"Prohibition meets the Cosa Nostra." She

slanted him a knowing look. "If not your club, then whose? Graeme's?"

He parked his truck between two nondescript sedans. "Apparently, we took the Roadhouse out of the mix for him."

"There's a mix?" Angel tapped the heel of her hand on the dash, considered. "This is just so not Graeme. Loves women, loves to party, but frequents dives and places where vampires might congregate? Not in the reality I know. You don't think there was more in Liz's journal than he told us, do you?"

"I think we should ask him the question." As he cut the engine, Noah nodded across the street. "Surveillance team vehicle belonging to Agents Warrick and Wickes. It's parked two cars down from Dr. Thomas's Mercedes."

Angel released a heartfelt sigh. "I should have gone to work for my uncle's whale-watching company."

HE WAS DRUNK, SO DRUNK that his head was on the table. Only his fingers moved, stroking the matte black top in time to a moaning saxophone.

Noah left Angel to rouse him while he spoke to the surveillance agents.

Setting her hands on his shoulders, she bent close and shook. "Graeme?"

His head snapped up, eyes bleary. "Who's there? Did something happen? Am I…" He regarded his fingers, wiggled them. "'S okay. Only a dream. Gotta look before I leap. Think." His head bobbed.

Angel shook him again. "Graeme."

"Stop bouncing the bed, Angel."

She grabbed a handful of his hair from behind. "Listen to me. I've had a pissy day, and I'm not in the mood to wrestle you back to your condo."

He offered up a crooked grin. "We'll just wrestle then. You and me. Still got your dark knight? Ask me, and I'll tell you how to lose a shadow. Go to a porno. Tiptoe to the can. Bye-bye. Back before the titillation's done. We're so weak…" His shoulders slumped. "Can I have more whiskey?"

With the last word, his eyes rolled up, and his neck muscles went limp. Noah appeared, gave his head a shake. "Forget it, Angel. He's cut."

"I hope you mean that in the alcoholic sense. If I'm right, it sounds like Graeme took our surveillance guys to a porno tonight."

"So they said."

"I think he ducked out on them."

"To do what?"

"Very good question. Wish I had a very good answer. Did they say how he was walking when the porno ended?"

"No, but Weekes thought he smelled booze when Graeme went past him. And he looked pissed off."

"Wonder why? Did you lose something?" she asked when he began searching his jacket pockets.

"Phone's vibrating."

"Phone? You got a replacement? When my cell broke, it took me three days to requisition another."

"You go through channels. I don't." He regarded the screen. "It's Pinkney. He must be trying to reach you through me."

"Slam-bang finish," she said and held out her hand. "Hey, Brian. What's up?"

"Me because of you. Charge your damn phone next time it dies. Bergman's been trying to contact you for the past two hours. There's another body on its way to the path lab. Pretty sure she's a Penny Killer victim."

Angel found a pen, used Graeme's drink napkin as a notepad. "Where and when?"

"In the alley behind the Muses, that derelict row of apartments scheduled for demolition in the spring. I don't have a time." He paused for effect. "We have witnesses, Angel. Three of them. Out of towners who got lost looking for an address. They saw a man loitering near the top of the alley."

"Do we have a description?"

"Don't need it. We have the loiterer. Liz is on-scene. Loiterer's in interrogation. I'm on my way downtown."

"Fifteen minutes, Bri." She listened for another few seconds then closed the phone. "Penny Killer victim, Noah, with potential suspect this time."

"Anyone we know?"

"Yeah." She handed back his cell. "Paul Reuben."

Chapter Twelve

"Are you the good cop or the bad cop, Angel?"

The reporter maintained a cocky veneer, but it was obvious to Angel that he was rattled by—well, any number of things. The victim's death, the fact that he'd run from the cops, or maybe that he'd been spotted at the murder scene by no fewer than three people.

She slid onto a hard chair across from him. "Until Liz gets back from the morgue, I'm both. You talked to Bergman already, yeah?"

"And his greasy lackey." Tipping his chair back, Reuben linked his fingers behind his head and spoke to the shadows. "Doing a rerun of the Invisible Man act, Graydon?"

"Depends on what you've got to say."

"Makes him the good cop by default." Reuben refocused on Angel. "I didn't do anything, didn't see anything."

"Just the woman's body, huh?"

"That's right. Body, blood and the contents of her purse scattered on the ground."

No wallet among those contents, Angel had been informed by Liz, but plenty of smudged fingerprints on the bag itself. "You got quite close to her then."

"Close enough to see what I saw."

"Why were you in the alley?"

"Why do you think? I got a tip."

He was trying to annoy her with his arrogant posture and the constant rat-a-tat-tat of his foot. Angel merely smiled. "From the Penny Killer?"

"Now how would I know that?"

"Before or after the murder?"

"Same answer."

"Either way, you come out looking like scum. Doesn't it bother you, Paul, that you might have prevented that woman's death simply by calling us with your tip?"

His expression might say screw you, but his arm muscles tightened visibly. "Not taking the bait, Angel."

"But you are comparing yourself to a fish. Speaks volumes to me." She glanced at the printout in front of her. "I see you bought a new cell phone."

"I'm allowed."

"Using your married sister's name."

"I'm giving it to her for Christmas. Wanted to check out the service first."

"How did your tipster get the new number?"

"You feds are monitoring my communication devices, you tell me."

Angel retained her amiable tone. "You know, Paul, even if you didn't kill that woman tonight, you can still be charged with obstruction of justice. Put a few bulldogs like Brian Pinkney on the case and chances are they'll manage to circumvent your flag-waving freedom of the press ride. I've seen it happen."

He yawned, but she noticed both feet were tapping now. "Can I go soon?" he asked.

Angel fixed a pleasant smile on her lips. "It's after midnight. Let's pretend, oh say, six hours have passed. We've run the circuit a hundred times. I ask, you insult. Okay, I'm getting nowhere. Next up, Brian Pinkney, then Bergman's assistant, then—well, who knows? We have dozens of 'bad cops' around here."

"Not scared yet, Carter."

"No? I think you are. Don't you think he is, Noah? He's got his fingers linked behind his head so we won't see them shaking."

Paul immediately lowered his hands to his lap. His grin became a sneer. "Am I really a suspect, or is this just you feds scrambling for a scapegoat?"

Angel's eyes sparkled. "No scapegoat needed, P.R. You're a full-fledged suspect. We found blood on both of your shoes and on the right cuff of your coat. Wanna bet it's the victim's?"

His lips compressed. For the first time, something like fear flitted across his face. "I didn't see her at first. You know as well as I do how far blood spurts when a major artery is severed."

"Good point. Won't knock you out of top spot on the short list, but you're right about blood. It gets everywhere." She angled her head, kept her expression benign. "Did you happen to see the victim's face, Paul? Liz did. She'd been crying. Word is she was planning a Christmas wedding. Maybe you think that sounds romantic. I did at first. But then Liz told me about a notation on her PDA. The woman had an appointment with her doctor tomorrow at 2:00 p.m. Her gynecologist. She was twenty-three years old, planning her wedding and ten weeks pregnant."

THEY COULD HOLD REUBEN for twenty-four hours. The next step depended on lawyer and judge.

By 5:00 a.m., Angel's brain had quite literally switched off. She spotted Noah, standing while he read a computer monitor in an empty office. Staggering over, she set her forehead on his back.

The next thing she knew she was drifting, far above Boston harbor on a silver cloud that transformed slowly into a silky bed of sand.

Had Noah taken her to the Cape? She thought he must have, because she could feel the ocean breeze on her face, taste the salty tang of it on her lips. It was warm, like summer, but even if it hadn't been, she wouldn't have cared. She was hot for the man whose mouth hovered tantalizing inches above hers on a dark and lovely dune.

She arched her neck, willed Noah to come to her this time. The demons were his to shed—or share if he could beat them back long enough to do that. Right now she'd be happy just having his mouth on hers, feeling him move inside her. Feeling his skin slide sleek and warm over hers.

"I want you, Angel," he murmured. "But there are things you need to know about my past."

What she needed was him, nothing more, nothing less. Why did he have so much trouble seeing that?

She nuzzled the corners of his mouth, let her fingers skim across his cheek, past the scar and over the patch that concealed his left eye.

He jerked, but didn't withdraw. "You want to see, don't you?"

"It won't make a difference to me, Noah."

"It might," he said and, lowering his head, let her lift the patch.

The light altered, struck the whole left side of his face. Angel gasped, dropped her hand.

"My God," she breathed. "Who did this to you?"

He pulled back as she'd known he would, emotionally more than physically. She tried to hold on, but he was already gone, into the shadows where he'd lived for far, far too long.

Regret consumed her, but backpedaling was pointless. "When did it happen?" she asked and saw his faint smile.

"When you'd expect. Five years ago. The same time the Penny Killer stopped killing."

When she reached for him, he caught her hand, held it. Tightly. "Don't feel sorry for me, Angel. I did this to myself. Fools rush in, and that's exactly what I did. Rushed headlong into a bloody knife. Lost an eye and part of my soul. But my loss was nothing next to the kid who lost his life that night." Relaxing his grip, he kissed her palm. "You don't want to get involved with me…"

The shadows shifted again. Light filtered through the dark. And he really was gone.

He was also wrong, so wrong she wanted to scream. Or cry. Or vent her frustration on the person responsible for so much pain.

Determined, she stood, headed for the cave where she'd seen him vanish. She would find Noah and make him understand, make him listen. She loved him, dammit, and nothing and no one could change that.

Halfway to the dark opening, she spied the creature, hobbling awkwardly and leering as it approached. It carried Brian Pinkney's knife under one wing and one of Paul Reuben's newspapers under the other.

And when it spoke, it did so with her father's voice…

"WAKE UP, ANGEL."

Fear like a wad of cotton stuck in her throat. Her

lungs hurt and she couldn't, simply could not, catch her breath. "Whoa!"

"Are you okay?"

It was almost too dark to see, but she could draw Noah's face from memory now. Clutching his arm with one hand, she pushed at her hair with the other. "Not sure. I think so." A shudder deep enough to rattle bone swept through her. "That was the worst for a long, long time." She closed her eyes, breathed with care. "So real."

"What happened?" He brushed strands of hair from her cheeks, brought her chin up. "Angel, what was it?"

She heard the concern in his voice, sensed his control.

"Bats. A bat. One." She held up a finger. Moscow, sitting on the bed beside her, promptly licked her hand. "I…" It suddenly hit her where she was, and she stopped. "How did I get home?"

"I drove you." Noah's grip on her nape was gentle but firm. And reminded her strongly about the good part of the dream. "You fell asleep in my truck. I didn't want to wake you, so I brought you up here and put you to bed."

"Really?" Surprise turned to pleasure, then back to surprise when she looked down and realized she was only wearing her bra and black bikinis. "Uh, who…?" She swept a hand over her body.

His lips curved. "You were out. It was like un-dressing a doll."

"Okay…" The dream crowded in again, and she gave a violent shudder. "It was horrible, Noah, worse than the elevator. My heart's still racing."

Noah grazed her cheek with his knuckle. "Where did this phobia come from?"

She shook free of the memory. "What? Oh, I got stuck in the loft of a neighbor's barn one night in Alaska. My father and his girlfriend came in and started making out. They didn't know I was there. The bats dropped out of the rafters and started limping toward me. I saw fangs and, in case you don't know it, they walk on their wings, which is about as creepy as it gets to a six-year-old. I swear, it seemed like there was a hundred of them. But I had to suck it up and be quiet, because if my father'd found me there, he'd have locked me in a room every night for a month with a whole bevy—bevy, flock, herd?—whatever, of them. I might have only been six, but I already knew one night of horror was better than thirty."

She noticed that his fingers tightened on her neck and tapped his wrist. "Don't be angry, Noah. He's a jerk, but my mom makes up for him." When Moscow licked her cheek, she smiled. "No objection, Agent Graydon, but what are you doing here?"

"I haven't had a chance to leave yet. I only brought you up five minutes ago."

"Which makes it what time?"

"Almost six."

"In the morning?" Groaning, she dropped her head onto his shoulder. "I have to be at work in three hours. Subtract prep and travel time, and that only leaves about ninety minutes for sleep." She inhaled the clean, soapy scent of his skin and hair and, shifting position, nipped lightly at his neck. "Or whatever else might spring to mind."

"You do this deliberately, don't you?"

Raising her head, she hooked her arms over his shoulders and set her mouth close to his. "Just a suggestion, Noah. Omitting the ending, there was a good side to that dream. We were on the Cape."

He ran his hands along her ribcage to her waist. "Were we alone on the Cape, or was someone watching us? Watching you? Stalking you?"

She frowned a little. "That's not a very romantic question considering that I'm mostly naked and you're sitting on my bed."

He half smiled. "I'll give you romance, Angel, and anything else you want. But you need to know what you're getting first." He stopped, brought his head around. "Did you hear something?"

"Only you trying to warn me off again." She set a finger on his lower lip. "I'm not fainthearted, and I'm the farthest thing from a femme fatale. I'm not easily shocked, and nothing you could possibly tell me about your past is going to upset me…" A low creak reached her, and it was her turn to pause. "Now that I heard."

So did Moscow. His ears went back, and he began to growl. "Stay," she told him and searched the darkened room for her clothes. "Noah?"

He was already off the bed with his gun out and angled toward the ceiling. "If I told you to let me handle this, would you listen?"

"I don't even listen to Bergman half the time." Angel located a pair of drawstring pants and a cotton T. How could someone have gotten past the security locks and into her condo? Checking her gun, she joined him at the door. "Did you set the alarm after you brought me in?"

"I thought it would make more sense to do that as I was leaving. Stay behind me."

"The Penny Killer doesn't come after his victims in their homes," she pointed out. "This could just be an intruder."

"Nothing dangerous about that, right?"

"Compared to a guy who's murdered ten people and threatened at least two more—no."

"Stay behind me," he repeated and made her want to jab his ribs. However, short of squabbling with him while someone prowled around her living room there wasn't much she could do.

Beside her, Moscow's muscles bunched. "No sound," she warned.

Another creak told her the intruder was making his way toward the window. Angel peered around Noah's arm. "The hall light switch is to your right."

"No lights."

"Noah, if he hears us and hides, he could blind-side us."

"Would you jump two armed feds?"

"Would I know I was in a fed's home? Quiet, Moscow. I'll go with your call, but if it backfires, remember I voted for light."

Noah eased his way down the corridor to the living room. The sounds had stopped. A night-light burned in the entry hall and a small lamp in her sunroom studio.

Angel used her gun to point. "I saw a movement over by my paint cabinet."

"On it. Stop whining, Moscow."

To Angel's amazement, the dog went silent. Said something about the man in front of her. What it said about Moscow, she wasn't sure. He didn't usually make noise when she told him not to.

She nudged Noah's back, but said nothing when the shadow shifted.

Was it the Penny Killer? Did he know she was here? Not know it? Realize Noah was with her?

Angel's heart rate accelerated. She acknowl-edged the rush of adrenaline but controlled it… Then the lamp went out.

"Can you see?" she whispered.

"As well as you."

She heard fabric rustle, spotted what appeared to be an arm. Holding a gun?

"Noah!"

He swung out to plant, and in the process created

a shield between her and the intruder. Moscow emitted a sharp yip. Angel brought her gun down.

When nothing happened, she frowned. "Where did he go?"

Noah regarded Moscow, then her studio. "Stay behind me," he said for the umpteenth time and made his way past the sofa to the studio opening.

A thud that sounded like a body hitting the floor had Angel snapping her gun up and Noah lunging forward to grab—someone.

Moscow's ears went up. He barked again and began to dance sideways.

The intruder gasped and grunted, then gave a short scream.

Unbelieving, Angel halted. Her arms fell. It took another grunt to get her moving again.

"Noah, stop!" She groped for the lamp over her easel. "It's not the Penny Killer." The light flared, illuminating all of them. "It's Liz."

"I'M SORRY, ANGEL, REALLY, really sorry about this."

Liz flicked her eyes in Noah's direction. Angel figured she could about half see him. Enough to realize that he was a stunning man, patch or not.

"I didn't think you were home. You usually park behind the building, and your spot was empty, so I used my key and came up to wait."

"I parked underground," Angel said. "It's closer to the front door... Liz, why are you here at six something in the morning?"

"I wanted to talk to you." Another brief eye flick. "About the case. Joe's still at the lab, so after I checked on Graeme, I came straight here."

Having hoisted himself onto the windowsill, Noah studied her from the shadows. "Do you want me to leave?"

"No." Liz removed the iPod ear buds she'd been using from around her neck. "I only wanted to go over some of the details while they were fresh in my mind. She—the victim—had a note. It was one of the few things still inside her purse. We missed it at first because she'd folded it with her electric bill. He used the back of a candy bar wrapper. The message said:

WALK IN MY SHOES
AS I WILL WALK IN YOURS
WHEN THE ANGEL FALLS
AND THE CIRCLE IS COMPLETE.

Angel disguised a chill. "Well, that's creepy."

She felt Noah's gaze on her. "He's repeating his message to you."

"Yes, I noticed that."

"Angel, he didn't kill that woman to reinforce the message. She's dead because he believes she should be."

"But I'm part of it," she countered. "I must be or why mention me in the note?"

"He's not going to get you."

"He couldn't, could he, so he got her instead." Because sitting was impossible, she paced a line back and forth behind the sofa. "What was her name, Liz?"

"Cori Baumgartner. She's William Baumgartner's daughter, his only child."

"Baumgartner." Something clicked in her memory. "Why do I recognize that name?"

"State Supreme Court Judge, William S. Baumgartner," Noah supplied. "He's been in the news recently. There were allegations that he accepted a bribe on a case he tried last summer. A handful of reporters were arrested when they attempted to break into his home."

"I remember the story. Ah…" A considering light sparked her eyes. "Wanna bet Paul Reuben was one of those reporters?"

"I'll go through the files."

Liz made a point of not looking at Noah. "I spoke to Cori's fiancé on the phone, Angel. Quick conversation, and he was understandably upset; but it's possible, in fact very likely, that he isn't the one who got her pregnant. She was ten weeks along according to her ob-gyn. But according to her fiancé, he only got back from Peru six weeks ago." She met Angel's eyes. "He'd been there for three months—while Cori was in Boston."

Chapter Thirteen

Joe was washing up when Noah arrived at the morgue-level lab.

"Welcome to the bowels of the bay." He dried his hands on a small towel. "Before you ask, this one was clean and tidy. No sign of a struggle, only a bit of bruising around the throat where he grabbed her. Left carotid sliced, down she went. No fuss, no—well." He gave an apologetic wave. "Sorry, I'm a little punchy today."

Noah picked up and scanned the report. "Any food down here?"

"Muffins and black coffee good enough?"

"Yeah." He kept scanning. "How are you and Liz?"

"Ships in the night at this point. Food's through here." Joe led the way. "Don't worry, there's a window between us and the body, and I covered her in any case."

Noah half smiled, glanced up. "It's me here, Joe, not Angel. You've set the time of death between 8:00 and 9:00 p.m."

"Best I could do. She was sick when she died, probably running a fever. Makes it harder to determine loss of body heat."

"It also says she was crying. Did the tears start before or after the killer grabbed her?"

"I'd say before. Her makeup was badly smudged, and she had a wadded up tissue in her hand. I won't go into detail, but some of the contents were tears." He nodded at the report while he poured coffee. "Proportions are there." He held up a muffin. "Nuked or not?"

"Not's fine. Was there anything uncharacteristic about the murder?"

"Not from this end. Liz was on scene. You can ask her."

Another glance as his friend handed him a muffin. "Did you get any sleep last night?"

"Not much." Joe flexed a shoulder. "I'll catch a few hours this morning and a couple more before I leave. Graeme's only been doing short stints at the Support Center lately, so I've had to take up the slack. Feels appropriate somehow when you consider what's going on around us. I'm told Lionel Foret's mother came by late yesterday afternoon. Stayed for an hour, told her tale, then got up and left in the middle of another family member's story."

"Did you talk to her?" Noah flipped to the second page of the report.

After topping his mug, Joe sank onto a stool.

"She's been in to the Center twice since coming to Boston, but not on my shifts. Graeme spoke to her once. He said she went on about Tweety Pie and some spider or other. He also smelled booze on her breath, which is the pot-kettle scenario, if you ask me. And I wouldn't have said that two weeks ago."

"Graeme's home now, right?"

"You Feds have a tail on him, you tell me."

"Guys are on him, yeah, but he won't let them inside his place. Weekes has requisitioned a van for the duration, says he's sick of playing caterpillar at night in Warrick's Ford Focus."

"Graeme went on a bender again last night, didn't he? No, don't answer. I got the story from Bergman's assistant. I think he enjoyed telling me about it. I'd also like to think it was an exaggerated account, but I have a feeling it wasn't, and for the life of me, I don't know what to do. It just isn't my brother to behave like this."

Noah set the report aside. "His life's been threatened, Joe. This could be a reaction to the note he got."

"Maybe." Joe rubbed badly bloodshot eyes, let his glasses fall back into place. "I try to think it through, then feel guilty when I don't reach the end because my mind veers off to Liz and that Peloni guy. 'Let it go, Joe,' you want to say. 'It was only a five-second phone call.' But if that's the case, Noah, why won't she talk to me about it? I'm wondering if I should give up my volunteer work at the

Center. Or maybe Liz should back off. One of us has to do something. You interested in doing a little pro bono moonlighting?"

"Helping families cope with the aftereffects of violent crime? Not sure I'd be much help to them, Joe."

"All you have to do is lend a sympathetic ear. Despite his party-hearty attitude, Graeme's excellent at that sort of thing. Liz, too, until recently."

"Has she been missing shifts?"

"Every second one, according to the director." Joe swirled his coffee. "It's funny, isn't it, how things can seem to be fine, going along well, in fact, then, bam, lightning strikes and your whole world's blown apart."

"She's not sleeping with Peloni."

"Man, I wish I believed that. There are times when I do. But then Graeme gets tanked, and I have to examine the body of someone who has no business being dead. And suddenly I realize life's nothing but a flip of the big coin. Heads you win, tails you lose."

What could he say? Coffee in hand, Noah nodded at the window. "Show me what you've got, Joe, and maybe we can flip the coin on the Penny Killer."

THE DAY DRAGGED, even though, thankfully, Bergman called and told her not to come in until two. Liz wouldn't talk, and Angel couldn't bring herself to pry. Wanted to, but they'd only been friends for eighteen months. Close or not, she hadn't earned the right to push that hard yet.

Paul Reuben walked from Holding at 4:00 p.m. His release incensed Cori Baumgartner's father. Turned out Reuben had led the journalistic assault on his estate last summer. He'd also written a blistering account of a trial which more than a few people had labeled "a complete mockery of justice."

As Angel understood it, a young man had died a brutal death. Eight months later, his killer had been freed on a technicality, one Baumgartner could have overridden in court but hadn't. In Baumgartner's view, the rules had to be obeyed, even when they conflicted with justice.

At 6:00 p.m., Angel and Liz had the unpleasant task of talking to Cori's fiancé. Upset? Oh, yes, he was that in spades, and adamant that the child Cori had been carrying was his. No way would she have tried to dupe him.

But Angel saw the glimmer of uncertainty in his eyes as they left, and her obstetrician's number jotted on a notepad beside the phone.

"I feel crappy," she said to Liz in the elevator, which, she took the time to note, had been inspected two months ago. "All we did was fuel that poor man's fears about Cori's fidelity."

"He talked to her doctor before we got there, Angel. The seeds of doubt were already planted. Do, uh, you have time to talk?"

Angel gave a careful nod. "I got six hours of sleep, and Mrs. Clausen brought up a pan of home-baked lasagna." She added a casual, "It was almost as good as Pete's."

Liz opened her mouth, closed it, then took a restless swing around the elevator. "Can I ask you something?"

"You know you can."

"Do you ever worry that you're doing the wrong thing?"

The laugh came automatically. "All the time. Why?"

"Are you worried about Graeme?"

"Yes."

"And Joe and me?"

"Slightly bigger yes."

"Do you think I'd cheat on him?"

"No."

Liz managed a wan smile. "That's a good-friend answer. Fast and definite. Thanks."

"You're welcome." Angel waited, let her eyes slide from side to side. "Anything else?"

"I think Joe's worried that Graeme knows more than he's telling about the Penny Killer."

"You—what?" Caught off guard, Angel stared. "Why would he think that? What would make him…?" She shook her mind clear. "Why?"

"I don't know. I just think he's worried. Maybe he's afraid Graeme stumbled across something, you know, accidentally."

"What kind of something? Liz, Graeme's about as far removed from our investigation as anyone in Boston can be. Paul Reuben might know more than he's admitting, and I'm not even a hundred percent sure about one or two of our coworkers, but…"

"You mean Brian?"

When the doors opened, Angel turned to walk backward so she could see her partner's face. "Do you know something?"

"I know he carries a knife in his sock. He was peeling grapes with it this afternoon."

"Well, yuck. He was stabbing dirty screws with it yesterday afternoon."

"Kind of give you the willies, doesn't it?"

"More than kind of."

Turning back around, Angel fastened her red leather jacket against the brisk wind that seemed to be blowing from all directions. "I think Brian and Noah have a history. It's not in the files, and no one in the office will comment on it, but there's something between them. Brian dislikes Noah, and I saw them talking in a dark room last night. It wasn't a friendly conversation. However," she swung to face Liz again, "that's a separate issue, and if I want to I can press Noah for details. We were talking about Graeme and what it is you think he knows about the Penny Killer."

"What, I have no idea. But I can tell you that shortly after Lionel Foret's murder, he was seen with Paul Reuben. They were in the clinic downstairs. Graeme was doing his monthly duty."

"And Paul was what? Reporter or patient?"

"Patient. Believe me, Angel, it took some fancy footwork, but I finally got Graeme to admit that he'd treated Reuben for a cut on his leg, a deep gash actually, as well as two fractured ribs. That's all he'd say—doctor-patient confidence, you know. But here's the thing. First he treated Paul, and that same night, he went out drinking."

"Can't Joe can't get anything out of him?"

Liz averted her gaze. "Joe's been busy lately. I know he's tried to talk to Graeme several times, but between home, work and the Center, time's thin— for all of us. Although he has been slacking off a bit lately."

"Graeme or Joe?"

"Graeme." Liz dipped her chin into the collar of her jacket. "And me."

Angel walked the rest of the way to the car in silence. Truthfully, she didn't know what to make of the information Liz had related. Did it pertain to the case? Or was the grape-peeling incident with Brian more significant?

Maybe Noah would be able to sort it out. She scanned the busy street, didn't see his truck. Didn't really expect to. But, as her mother said: "Look for a frog, you'll find a frog. Look for a prince, you might still find a frog. Look for nothing, and your prince will come."

Liz heaved out a breath. "I was thinking that Joe might like a home-cooked meal for a change. What do you think?

Angel grinned. "That we're five minutes from Little Italy, and I have a craving for more pasta. Drop me at Fortino's, then go home and make your kids and hubby happy. I'll cab it to my place."

Liz glanced away. Toward Peloni's? "I guess I could do that. Promise you'll go straight home? No alley, farm or tearoom detours?"

Angel made a cross over her heart. "I want a glass of wine, a bubble bath and Ella on my iPod."

Liz unlocked the car. "I think you want a whole lot more than that, Angel. And I'm more than sure he'll want to oblige."

"Hope so." Angel felt her phone vibrating, pulled it out and regarded the screen. "Caller unknown. It's probably Bergman's lackey. I've heard he has at least ten phones so he can ambush agents day and night. Carter," she answered.

"Ah, Angel…" A distorted voice rattled back at her. "We speak at last. Did you think I'd forgotten you? Do you feel neglected? Unimportant? Overlooked? I assure you, you're none of those things. The circle closes with your death. I've waited so long for this moment. Oh, my beautiful Angel, it will be sweet justice. Sweet, sweet justice at last."

ANGEL SAID NOTHING to Liz—and wasn't entirely sure why. It amazed her that she could pull off a credible cover-up, but she knew she'd succeeded when Liz deposited her at Fortino's as planned, repeated her earlier warning and left with a honk of the horn.

She wandered through the Italian grocery store, picking items off the shelves while she shook off the aftereffects of the call. The computer-altered voice had chilled her, to be sure, but it wasn't as if she hadn't expected the killer to make good on his threat. It was more that time and distance had given her a false sense of security. He'd been ignoring her, more or less, since that attack in the alley. Foolish of her to have grown so complacent.

She finished her shopping on autopilot, purchasing, among other things, Chianti, gnocchi and a Boston cream pie—because people under threat of death deserved to indulge.

One thing she knew, she needed to remain calm in order to think clearly. Stay in the zone, and she could cope. Step out, and she'd be exactly where the killer wanted her. One slash away from death.

She spied Noah's truck when her taxi pulled up in front of her building. She also noticed fog that hadn't been there earlier, slippery gray ribbons that slunk around her ankles as she crossed the street.

Noah got out, dropped his cell phone in the pocket of his coat and would undoubtedly have said something if Angel hadn't ditched her bags, fisted his hair and yanked his mouth onto hers.

"Don't want to talk," she told him between kisses. "Just want to feel."

Which she did, for several long seconds, and, oh God, it was good. Diverting. Delicious. Exactly what she needed to bolster her flagging defenses.

He accepted the challenge without comment or question. Possibly without thought, either, because the heat came in a finger-snap flash that surprised even her.

Angel wanted to jump up and wrap her legs around him, to take and give far more than she'd first planned.

Kiss him, she'd thought. Obliterate the horror and the fear. Get lost, just for a moment, in the dark, brooding mystery of the man.

"Angel…"

"Talk later," she repeated and felt his lips curve against hers.

"Yeah, I got that part. Your bags…"

There were only two and she bent just far enough to slide them over her wrists. Then she draped her arms over his shoulders.

"Any more objections?"

"It wasn't an objection."

"Good, then…"

Noah cut her off this time, with a kiss that stripped the air from her lungs and made the blood shoot like liquid fire through her veins.

As always, his tongue did unbelievable things to her mouth. Then he swept her into his arms and brought a purr to her throat.

"You really are a dark knight." She nipped at him in a blatant tease, let her tongue soothe the sting. "Dark knight with strong arms, a big sword and an air of mystery that just won't quit."

"I thought you said no talk."

"So I did," she agreed and attacked his mouth again.

Subtle pot lights in the corridor and stairwell danced in her head. Beneath his clothes, Noah's body felt hard to her exploring hands. His hair was black silk, his skin sleek satin. And the taste of him was far more intoxicating than the Chianti she'd bought. It was pure, raw sex.

Need curled inside her. Hunger laced through it. Wriggling slightly, Angel got him to release her legs so she could wrap them around his hips.

Much better position, her fevered mind decided. More direct contact. She could feel his full arousal now and revel in the knowledge that he wanted her as much as she wanted him.

It might have started with a voice on the phone, but it wouldn't end there. Couldn't. Not when every nerve in Angel's body was screaming for satisfaction.

Noah disarmed her security system between kisses. She dumped the groceries and her jacket, started tugging at his coat.

The sultry jazz music was ready-made and appropriate, filling the air from the stereo she left playing to keep Moscow company during the day. While the shadows slanted and stirred, Rosemary Clooney sang a torchlight song.

Fog thickened the darkness outside. Angel thought of a transatlantic ship—no idea why—of cool nights, ocean swells and a saxophone crooning just for them.

Another gentle wriggle, and her feet hit the floor. She dragged the coat from Noah's shoulders, began working on his jeans. Stubborn catch first, then the fly. She wanted to feel his erection, skin to skin. Heat to need.

It was all about sensation now. His mouth slid over her jaw and cheek, into her hair. That's when she felt it, the faintest of hesitations.

"Angel…"

"Later," she promised. "After."

She thought for a suspended moment that he might pull away as he had in her dream. As he had in so many dreams. But the moment passed, and with a sound of pure male desire, he covered her mouth with his.

Angel tugged at his T-shirt, blood red today, and drew him toward her bed. His skin was volcanic beneath her hands. She explored his chest and shoulders, ran her palms over his upper arms, then back to his chest and ribs and across his stomach.

She felt sinew and taut, hard muscle. She felt his

arousal pressing into her lower body, found it amusing that her own clothes had managed to disappear without her noticing. Son of an amateur magician indeed. What other illusions might he pull out and use?

No, not illusions, enhancements. Because all of this was real. It was what she'd been waiting for, what she'd been wanting, for longer than she could remember.

His fingers drew a slow, sly line across her belly. A quiver of anticipation jittered through her. A shudder followed. Quick, hard and fierce enough to make her jolt.

"You all right?"

She smiled against his lips. "Not sure." Then nuzzled the corners. "Do that again."

Her fingers tangled in his hair, though she was careful not to dislodge the patch over his eye. Like talk, that was for later, for when the blood wasn't boiling inside her like mercury on fire.

Easing back just far enough to speak, he chuckled. "Mercury on fire, Angel?"

"I have the soul of a very bad poet." Touching her tongue to her upper lip, she let her hands run from stomach to pelvis to groin.

Swearing softly, Noah kicked off his unfastened jeans.

His skin gleamed in the eerie city glow that trickled through the window. Angel kept her eyes on his face as he lowered her onto the bed.

She didn't want to let go, and didn't have to, because he rolled her over and pinned her to the mattress.

Need swamped her from head to toe. Thought fled. She arched her hips against him, took him in her hands and simply let herself savor.

It was a wild upward spiral, unlike anything she could have anticipated. With every heartbeat, words thrummed in her head. More. Harder. Faster…Now!

"It's too soon," he murmured. "We need to slow down."

"You think?" Kissing him again, she wrapped her fingers around his throbbing erection and brought him deep inside her.

It was an explosion, a blast of heat and light, of color and sound, swirled together in a fiery pool that sucked her right into its living center. It was skin on skin, burn on burn. It was Noah inside her, driving himself deeper, and deeper, and deeper.

The sexual rush overwhelmed her. Angel's head pushed down into the pillow. A cry rose in her throat. Her fingernails bit into his hips as she met him thrust for thrust.

The climax hit hard and fast, sweeping over and through her in a burst of white light that tore the breath from her lungs and every thought from her head. She saw sparks, she swore she did, little zaps of electricity that sensitized her nerve ends and left her feeling wonderfully alive. Not so much alert, because the carousel in her brain continued to spin at top speed, but more aware than she'd been in years—of anything, or anyone.

Blood pounded in her ears. She couldn't move, could barely breathe. "Need air, Noah, now. Really, seriously need air."

Noah merely grunted out a sound and collapsed on top of her. Which did amazing things to her zinging metabolism but nothing to alter the oxygen situation.

Thank God he rolled, because she couldn't have pushed for the life of her, might never be able to connect brain-to-muscle function again.

"And so we mate." She closed her eyes. "And die." Her body felt limp, right down to her bones. "I wish I thought it would all end this way. Who could fear moving on if this was the send-off?"

"I thought you were an optimist," he said into her hair.

"I am, and that was. When I die, this is how I want to go. A big bang, followed by a fantastic slow slide."

"Slides go down, Angel. Pretty sure you won't in the end."

She almost had the strength to laugh. "I know people who'd argue that, but I'll leave it alone and devote my energy to the revivification process. Because…" She slid a hand between them, made Noah groan and herself grin. "I'm a greedy sort of person. I want to do it again. And again. And again."

"In which case we'll both be dead by dawn."

"Oh much sooner than that," she promised and turned her mouth to his. Her eyes sparkled. "I hope your will's in order, Graydon."

FOG FROM THE HARBOR hazed the edges of the building. Had it hazed her fear as well? She was up there now, in the dark, with the very person whose fault it was that her life must end.

A child could understand why, and so would Angel if she'd simply adjust her thinking and approach the matter from the proper angle.

Curled fingers slowly uncurled. Fury stuttered and ebbed. One way or another, the end was in sight, at long last, a mere double-fisted victory cry away.

Angel Carter would die. Noah Graydon would watch.

And, when it was done, when the circle was complete and forever sealed, of three who came together, only one would walk away.

Chapter Fourteen

"So you do know Brian Pinkney?" Lying on her side, with her head resting in her hand, Angel fingered Noah's hair. "Not so much as a coworker from when you first came to Boston, but as the bearer of a large and still-not-quite-clear-to-me grudge."

Fog continued to curl outside the bedroom window. Five scented candles inside cast a warm glow over the two personal canvases she'd deemed worthy enough to hang on her walls. Rosemary had given way to Ella, Moscow dreamed happy dog dreams in his corner bed, and after making love three times, she and Noah were on their tongue-loosening third glass of Chianti.

"You hungry?" Noah asked while she sipped. "For food," he added at the teasing tilt of her brows.

"I am, yes, but not enough to let you off explaining your relationship with Brian. Story first, gnocchi later. Trust me, Noah, Fortino's pasta is well worth a few minutes of talk."

His expression grew wry. "No story involving Brian and me is, was or ever could be told in a few minutes."

"So I'll help you out. How did you meet—when, where, etc?"

"Through a coworker in DC, eight years ago."

"Were you friends?"

"Not remotely, but we had a mutual friend. Jerry Kraus."

Angel stopped ruffling his hair, set her palm on his chest. "That name rings an even louder bell than Judge Baumgartner's. Kraus." She drew a slow circle on Noah's stomach. "Wasn't he the agent who…? No, couldn't be."

"It could, and it was."

Her expression went from considering to genuinely surprised. "The guy who murdered his entire family—wife, kids, in-laws—you were friends with that Jerry Kraus?"

"Worse, we stood up for him in court. Brian and I were called as character witnesses."

"But that's not possible." She thought back. "After he murdered his family, Kraus killed himself."

"That was several months later. What I'm talking about was more of an internal hearing. It only read like a trial after the murder-suicide."

"What did this hearing-that-read-like-a-trial entail?"

"Two federal prisoners accused Jerry of physically abusing them while they were in custody. One claimed he was responsible for breaking three ribs. The other said he caused a concussion."

"What did you and Brian do?"

"We told the federal investigation board what we knew. As far as we'd seen, Jerry had never lost control in any way. Not with us, not with his family, not with anyone he'd interrogated or brought in."

"But?"

Noah's shadowed gaze shifted from her face to the window. "Somewhere in the back of our heads, I think we both had questions about the guy. Unfortunately, what we saw on the surface was an upstanding, and in many ways outstanding, federal agent, a great family man and a good friend."

"Who sadly had a silent monster living inside him."

"The mother of monsters, Angel. Based largely on our testimony, the allegations against him were dismissed, the investigation dropped. Five months later, seven people were dead."

"Sometimes monsters are like that, Noah." Sympathy swept in. "Please tell me you don't blame yourself for what happened to Kraus's family."

But the set of his features told her he did. "We stood up for him. I stood up for him."

"You answered questions to the best of your knowledge. You're punishing yourself for being honest. That's—" she searched for the word she wanted, but couldn't find anything more appropriate than "—wrong. It's just plain wrong."

"So was I."

"But you didn't think you were. And Brian, who's a completely different person than you, gave the same character reference. To me that says Jerry Kraus was an excellent actor—which, as you've told me repeatedly, many sociopaths and murderers are."

"They are, and he was, but the bulk of the blame still falls on me. I was the more prominent agent back then. My word carried more weight."

Angel set her chin on his shoulder. "You're saying that because you want the burden of guilt to lean more heavily in your direction than in Brian's. But the point is, neither of you did anything wrong." She released a long breath, raised her head. "Still, having said that, I'll admit I'd feel exactly the same way. What was the board's reaction?"

"No reaction beyond a lot of gritted teeth and a truckload of spin doctors positioned front and center to ensure that the integrity of the Bureau wasn't damaged beyond its ability to self-repair."

"As most levels of government and the justice system do on a daily basis. Look at Judge Baumgartner, Noah. He allowed a murderer to go free. Why? Because the warrant used by the police wasn't totally in order. I mean, get real, I read the transcript of the trial. Judge Baumgartner was nitpicking to the max. My grandfather told me something about British justice once. Probable cause is all the police there need to go in, sans warrant, and search a suspect's home."

"Obviously, you're not a believer in the expression 'Justice will out.'"

"I prefer Justice for all. I suppose in a twisted sort of way, and adding the word 'poetic' to the term, Baumgartner got a measure of that when Cori was killed. He'll certainly understand now how the families of the murderer he freed must feel… And no, what the judge did and what you and Brian did are not the same things."

"Did I say they were?"

"Your face did. I'm getting very good at reading your expressions in shadow light. My point is, Noah, that you weren't in a position to speculate regarding Jerry Kraus. Judge Baumgartner had far more power to control and, well, judge, and yet he screwed up. Not that I don't feel very deeply for him and even more so for Cori, but he is on the other end of it now, and maybe, God help him, if he's ever in a similar situation to the one he bungled, he'll see things a little differently."

"You have strong views, Angel."

"Comes from too much alone time as a child. Anyway, soapbox speech done. Climbing down and getting back on topic. The story is that you and Brian have a rather macabre link. You blame yourself for standing up for a man who turned out to be a mass murderer, and knowing Brian, he blames you as well. On the surface, at least. My guess is he feels a similar sort of guilt inside…" She tapped a speculative finger on Noah's chest. "Unless I'm as off the mark as your investigative board, and that knife Brian carries in an ankle strap really belongs to another hidden monster."

To her surprise, Noah's lips curved into a vague smile. "Not that I'm a fan of the man, but I wouldn't devote much time to the 'monster inside' theory where Pinkney's concerned."

"And you say that because?"

Noah's unpatched eye glinted. Not with humor, she realized, but with something much darker. "Oh, damn." She let her head fall forward. "There's more, isn't there? Why is there always more?"

"Nature of the human beast, Angel. We're complex creatures, and that complexity infects our lives, our involvements and our problems."

"Which somehow translates to, Brian's unlikely to be the Penny Killer." Giving Noah's chin a pinch, she leaned closer. "Okay, 'splain the why of it to me, Graydon."

"In a nutshell? You have a fed on your list of PK victims, yeah? His name was Steve Oakland."

"He was the last victim before the Penny Killer went on—well, hiatus, I guess you could say." Suspicion kindled. "As it happens, Oakland's file is the sketchiest of the group. It also contains the greatest number of locks, ones Bergman insists have no bearing on the current investigation."

"They don't," Noah agreed. "You have what you need. Steve was green, smart as hell, but still in training. He let himself be drawn into a trap. By the time his trainer realized what he'd done, it was too late. The kid was caught."

Sensing she'd need it, Angel shifted position so she could pour them both more wine. "You were Oakland's trainer, weren't you?"

He slid his gaze over her shadowed breasts, brought a slow flush to her already warm skin.

A smile grazed her lips as she handed him his glass. "Play later," she said softly. "Finish your story first."

"I wish it was a story." Noah swirled, drank. "Oakland had smarts and drive and, unfortunately, something to prove. He got a line on the Penny Killer, but instead of telling anyone about it, he went in alone. I found out where he'd gone fifteen minutes after he left for a harborside warehouse.

"The place was burning when I got there," he continued. "Steve was dead, but I saw the killer heading for the waterfront door. It was mid-winter, dark and the blizzard that was blowing had pretty much shut the city down earlier in the day. I went after the guy, actually caught him when he tripped over a crate."

"You caught the Penny Killer?"

"Caught hold of him. I was prepared to knock

the knife from his hand. So prepared that I missed the gun."

"Oh, God."

"My thought exactly." Taking her hand, he set it over a small scar on his ribs. "Other side and I'd have been dead. PK pulled the trigger while I was going for his mask."

"He wore a mask?"

"Ski mask. Black wool. Fiber told us nothing, and I doubt he wore it on a regular basis. He was pulling it on when I spotted him, probably had it with him because of the blizzard."

In her mind, Angel only saw blood. Noah's blood, seeping over the floor of a burning warehouse.

"Oakland's file said he didn't burn in the fire," she recalled. "You got him out, didn't you?"

"Eventually. Right then, I was still fighting with the guy who'd killed him. But I was also losing blood, and we both knew it. I managed to kick both his knife and his gun away. We kept fighting. He got in a solid hit, got hold of the knife, slashed me." Noah drew a line from the top of his eye patch to the tip of the scar on his cheek.

Angel wanted to trace that same line with her own fingers, but was afraid he'd pull away, so she set a hand on the scar left by the bullet and waited for him to finish.

"That's all I remember," Noah told her in a tone that suggested he'd gone over this countless times past and present. "I found Oakland, dragged him out and collapsed beside him in the snow. Next thing I knew, I was waking up in the hospital. Steve was dead, my eye was gone, and one of the nurses told me that Brian Pinkney was having spinal surgery. Consensus was the killer got trapped in the warehouse and died in the fire."

Angel struggled with a shiver for the blood she couldn't seem to get out of her head. "Obviously an invalid assumption. And I missed the segue, Noah. How was Brian tied to what went down that night?"

"He was en route when he crashed his vehicle into a freeway median."

"Next question—why was he en route? Unlike you, he wasn't listed as being part of the original investigation team. For that matter, neither was Steve Oakland."

"Killer sent Oakland a note."

"Ah." Comprehension dawned, but faded to confusion. "And Brian?"

"Got a last-minute tip about the warehouse. He wasn't part of the team—which had pissed him off from the start—but he'd been keeping an eye on the investigation anyway."

"And now the bombshell, right?"

Noah's faint smile warned of something more ironic than shocking. "I told you Oakland had something to prove, possibly to someone other than himself, and I was right. He wanted to show

Brian what he could do, how good an agent he could be."

Inevitability struck like a blow to Angel's midsection. "They were related."

Noah's gaze traveled to the window before returning to her face. "Brian didn't know it until the day Steve showed up in DC for training. I guess the kid marched right in and told him. He was going to prove to Agent Pinkney what he was made of. Steve had known all his life what Brian only discovered that morning. Steven Oakland was Brian Pinkney's son."

THEY ATE GNOCCHI AND Boston cream pie, talked a little more and made love again. Twice. In the back of her mind, Angel's opinion of the Brian she'd known for eighteen months mellowed to something a little more compassionate.

Whether he deserved compassion or not, she couldn't say. But if the idea of his son confronting a killer in a harborside warehouse had caused him to crash his vehicle, he must have cared to some extent, even if it was twenty-three years after the fact.

It wasn't until the fog began to slink out of the city toward the bay that she finally told him about the phone call she'd received the previous afternoon. His response...?

"He didn't take it quite as well as I'd hoped," Angel confessed to Liz hours later over a later-than-usual lunch. "He got dressed, put on his coat, took me by the arms and kissed the hell out of me. Then he gave me one of those 'I'm really pissed off' looks he's better at giving than anyone I know, and left."

"Says 'love' to me, partner. Now read my pissed off look." Arms crossed, hip resting on the deli counter, she glowered at Angel. "Message getting through that thick skull of yours yet?"

"Received and processed." Angel indicated the Reuben sandwiches, held up two fingers for the counterman. "Maybe I should have told both of you first thing, but guess what?" She waved a hand in the air between them. "Professional here. There was nothing either of you could have done that I didn't do. I tried for a trace. No luck. Call was made from a pay phone outside a downtown movie theater. The voice was altered and unrecognizable. I'm guessing the message was pre-recorded. All I can tell you is that it sounded like a guy, which we already know the killer is, so wow, startling revelation. You'd have obsessed all night, Noah would have freaked, and let's face it, partner, it isn't as if you aren't keeping a secret or two from me."

Liz's expression went from annoyed to accepting to defensive. She squeezed her wrapped sandwich. "I don't know…"

"What I'm talking about?" Angel paid the cashier, took her own sandwich and started out. "I think you know exactly what I mean, and so would Pete Peloni. Oh, no, wait." She executed a half spin. "I forgot, Pete Peloni's dead. He fell into a dried up Texas well three years ago."

Liz's eyes closed. "Angel... Oh, crap." She swore as her phone rang. "Thomas," she answered in an irritable voice that tweaked a cord of guilt in Angel's mind. This wasn't how she'd wanted to approach Liz where Pete was concerned.

Her own cell began to vibrate, and with a glance at the screen, she opened it. "Hi, Brian. News?"

"Maybe." He sounded stiff. "A police patrol found Cori Baumgartner's wallet in a Dumpster eight blocks from where she died. Cash was gone, but her credit cards were still inside. We didn't get any clear fingerprints from the purse, but the lab guys salvaged one from the wallet."

"Please tell me this is going to move the investigation forward, Bri."

"Best I can say is that the print belongs to a greasy piece of street slime, affectionately known to the city cops as Hobo. Used to be Ho Bo—two separate nicknames, if you take my meaning—when the guy was younger and more of a stud. But thirty years later, the altered name fits like a dirty glove. You getting my drift here, Carter?"

"Drumming my fingers on the roof of the car and waiting for the meat."

Her coworker grunted. "Slime's in Holding. Bergman wants you to question him. Figures you have a warm enough approach to melt through the decades of street crust."

"I'm touched. Be there in ten." She closed her phone, regarded Liz, whose expression fell somewhere between mutinous and miserable. "Problem?"

"My new nanny just quit."

"Oh." Because she'd been expecting something different, a bubble of laughter swelled. "I'm, uh, sorry."

Liz glared. "You don't look it."

"I know, and I'm sorry about that too, because I really do feel for you. I also know this puts you in a difficult position. I don't suppose Joe's home today."

"No, and the hospital's been calling all morning. They can't track Graeme down. My brother-in-law has a liver transplant pending, so what does he do? Takes off to God knows where. A donor liver could become available any time. The surgeon, not so much."

All amusement died. "I'm really sorry about this, Liz, and I mean all of it. Go. Deal with the nanny and your kids. I can question a thirty-year street veteran, no problem—my call," she added. "But you have to promise me we'll talk about Pete, and why the hell he's impersonating a dead man."

Liz searched for her keys. "We'll talk, Angel, we will." She caught her partner's arm. "Just you promise me that you won't approach him alone."

Angel felt a stirring of unease. "Is he dangerous?"

"Promise me," Liz repeated.

"I—okay, I promise. But you…"

"I'll explain." Liz set her mouth in a grim line. "Then I'll accept the consequences of my actions."

Chapter Fifteen

It took three frustrating hours of parrying with Bergman's assistant to finally extract Hobo from Holding, another ninety minutes to coax coffee down his resistant throat and thirty more to get him into a witness room.

Just as well, Angel decided, that she and Liz had eaten such a late lunch, because she couldn't see leaving here for several more hours. Braced for the smell and another verbal spar, she opened the door.

With his gray head hovering just above the tabletop, Hobo squinted at her. "Back again, huh, cutie? Wanna shoot a game of pool? I got cash."

"Such a charmer." Smiling, Angel took a seat across from him. "Word is you scored a nice fat wad of greenbacks."

He flapped a filthy hand. "Easy pickin's. Came up from Timmy's hideout 'cause I needed to take a leak. You know how it is."

"Don't we all?"

He took a conspiratorial look around, before

stretching across the table to whisper, "Anyways, there's this girl and this guy, and he's huggin' her from behind, right? Thought they was gonna…" He trailed off and blinked several times as if he'd suddenly clued in. "Wait a minute. You a cop?"

"And here we go." Angel pulled a large covered tray between them. "Okay, here's the deal, Ho."

"Call me Bo, cutie." He went to prop his chin in his hand, missed and almost crashed to the table. "Slippery sucker. What was I saying? Oh, ya, Bo. Lost the Ho part long time ago. Talk slow so's I don't get fuddled, 'kay?"

"How about you talk and I'll listen. Then maybe you'd like a nice hot dinner, hmm?" She fingered one of the plate covers. "Steak, mushrooms, roasted potatoes, blueberry pie for dessert. Oh, and cigarettes, too. Couple packs of them. Not a healthy choice, but better given than stolen, yeah?"

Hobo all but drooled when she tipped up the lid on the steak.

"What d'you want to know, cutie?"

She slid him a cigarette, matchbook and ashtray. "Have an appy and tell me about the night you saw the man hugging the woman from behind. Come through with anything useful, dinner and smokes are yours. More than useful, we'll put you up for a night in a decent flop."

He showed cracked, brown teeth. "You like poker better 'n pool, don't you?"

Not quite so drunk now, she noted. "I like all

kinds of games. Real good at spotting bluffs. Talk to me, and door number one here is all yours."

Eyes closed, he ran the cigarette under his nose. "No strings? Cops always have strings."

"I'm not a cop. The guy I'm after kills, Bo. Men and women, with homes and without. He's not fussy, and he's not into deals. If he realizes you saw him with that woman, he'll be on you like a one-man firing squad. Savvy?"

"Kinda." He lit up, puffed, savored. "You're talking fast."

"How about I stop and you start. What happened after he hugged the woman?"

Hobo's grubby features screwed themselves into a mask of concentration. "Blood came out. Squirted so far it hit the wall."

"Were you behind him?"

Ashes scattered as he gestured backward. "Ya, by the garbage cans."

"Could you see his face?"

"Nope."

"Describe something else about him then. Was he tall, short, thin, fat, bald, hairy—what?"

"Taller 'n me."

"And you're, what, five-six?"

"Seven." Still somewhat pie-eyed, he took a short detour down memory lane. "Wore cowboy boots and a hat in my heyday. Ladies loved the hat. So what I'm not Tom Selleck? You wanna talk Toms, that Tom Cruise…"

"Has no bearing on this case. Concentrate, Bo. What color was the guy's hair?"

"Have to think. He stayed mostly in the shadows. Maybe brown."

"Long or short?"

"Collar was up. Couldn't tell."

"The collar of his coat or jacket?"

"Coat. Black, long, you know, like spies wear."

"A trench?"

"If that's what spies wear. Had gloves on, too. Black." He smoked the cigarette down to the filter. When it fizzled out, he set it in the ashtray as if laying an old friend to rest. "It happened awful fast. Bim, bam, boom, she's on the ground. Guy kneeled down, stuck something on her face, pulled out a handkerchief and vamoosed... Or, no, other way 'round. First he wiped his own face, then he did the rest."

Angel gave him another cigarette. "Can you describe the handkerchief?"

"Nothing special. Had blue and white checks on it, and it was all big and wrinkled." His expression of bliss as he sniffed the tobacco was interrupted by a sudden frown. "Oh, ya, and he said something like, 'Take that, pudge.'" Shrugging, he returned to bliss. "Not that she was fat. Kinda skinny, y' ask me. Can I have a potato?"

Angel nudged a fork toward him and tilted the aluminum lid. "Take two and think hard. What else did you see or hear?"

Hobo chewed loudly, then subsided and lit up. "Said something I couldn't hear so good 'cause of the handkerchief. It was like, 'Now you know how—something, something.' 'Cept he wasn't talking to her. Did I say that before? He was looking somewheres else. Almost dropped his knife."

"You saw a knife?"

"Well, he didn't cut her with his fingernail."

In her jacket pocket, Angel's phone vibrated. Be Noah, she willed, but of course, it wasn't. She let Hobo nab another potato, debated over the words 'caller unknown', then shook it off and answered.

"Carter."

"Oh, you are a good little agent, Angel."

The sound of the distorted voice set her teeth on edge. "I'm not afraid of you," she told him.

"Yes, I know." Not prerecorded this time. "But you'll be a very sorry woman if you don't listen and do exactly what I tell you. Are you listening?"

"Yes."

"I have your lover, Noah Graydon. Deny that he's your lover, and he dies. Don't come to me, same result."

Angel's blood turned to ice water. "Where are you?"

She heard silk under the distortion, triumph layered over anticipation. "Oh, Angel, this is the moment. At long last, you'll know me. Both of you will know me. Come to me, Angel. Come to us. Do I have to say 'alone'? I'm at Brogan's farm. I have your lover's cell phone in my hand. It rings, he dies. Since I don't know where you are, I'll be generous and give you an hour to get here. Drive safe, Agent Carter."

Angel closed the phone, steadied her breathing. A bluff, or reality? She couldn't be sure and didn't dare call Noah to find out. One way or another, though, she had to believe he'd survive. The killer wouldn't harm him. Noah knew how to take care of himself.

So why, she wondered with a shiver, did she keep seeing a river of blood outside an old warehouse?

"I have to go, Bo." Shoving back, she fired him the cigarette pack. "I'll send another agent in. You can talk to him."

"Don't wanna talk to a him." Hobo smirked. "Like you better."

"Close your eyes. Pretend he's me."

As the cigarettes disappeared into his pocket, a crafty look appeared on Hobo's face. "I was just getting to the good part, cutie."

It would take her forty minutes to reach Brogan's farm. Thirty-five if she pushed it. Thirty if she abandoned all caution.

"Okay, talk."

"Hotel for a week?"

"Or maybe obstruction of justice instead. You have your deal and about fifteen seconds."

"He dropped the handkerchief."

Her eyes sharpened. "Do you have it?"

"Nope. Did I say it was wrinkled and mostly blue?"

"I'm leaving, Bo."

"Saw it best when it fell in the blood," he went on. "But I guess maybe he didn't notice, 'cause that's when he kneeled down and did something to the dead girl's face. Then I saw, thought I saw, someone coming down from the other end of the alley. Got a bit antsy."

She hesitated on the threshold. "And then?"

"Well, the guy who did her ran, didn't he?"

"With or without the handkerchief?"

"Without."

"But you don't have it."

Hobo followed her eyes to the clock. Treating her to a cracked-tooth smile, he used the index finger of his cigarette hand to tap his forehead. "Don't have the handkerchief, but I got a face."

"Hobo, you said you didn't see…"

He waved her off. "Forget before. I had to know what was in it for me, didn't I? Deal's okay. Face is in my head." The smile became a canny chuckle. "How's 'bout now I put it in yours?"

"How could you lose him?" With a side-to-side look into the misted shadows, Noah strode up the walk to Graeme's condo. He nabbed a man who was exiting through the front door and showed his FBI badge. "We need to get in."

The startled man fumbled his key back out and reopened the door. Agent Weekes trailed along in Noah's wake, his expression sheepish but determined.

"If the guy chooses to sneak out on us, that's his business, Graydon. We're here for his safety, not because he's a suspect."

Noah scanned the elevator lights. Beside him, he felt Weekes subtly angling for a clear view at his face. "Wait down here. Thomas might come back. Tell Warrick to stay on the parking lot."

He shoved through the stairwell door before Weekes could object and made the seven-flight climb two steps at a time, cursing himself all the way.

The surveillance team guesstimated that Graeme Thomas had vanished sometime after 7:00 p.m. At least that was the last they'd seen of him.

As they had for the better part of the day, Noah's thoughts moved back and forth between facts and conjecture. The constant flipping jarred. It wasn't his way to be so unfocused.

He'd have blamed Angel, except that wasn't his way either. Besides, being with her, talking to her, making love with her, had only made things better. In some strange way, it had almost made them right.

So where did the disorder and the black mood stem from? What lurked in the back of his head that made him want to put five rounds of bullets into a practice target?

At Graeme's door, he used the code Angel had given him earlier that week to disengage the alarm.

Instinct, and an unofficial call from Bergman, had driven him here after hours of computer work. He'd read the notes received by the past and present victims. He'd typed in names, drawn lines, dissected, bisected and when necessary stitched together. In the end, it was the latest deviations that stood out most clearly.

None of Luki Romero's three living spaces had yielded a note. Luki could have received and destroyed his, certainly that was possible. But it was also the easy answer, and it didn't feel right.

The word "justice" flashed like a neon sign in his brain. Angel had talked about it this morning, and he'd been thinking it ever since. No idea why. With the exception of Luki, there was no sense of justice being carried out through any of the Penny Killer murders. And, unlike his brother, Luki didn't even have a record.

Which meant what?

Noah felt certain the answer had been dangling in front of him for some time, yet something about the angle rendered it invisible to everyone but the killer.

As he rifled through cupboards and drawers, Noah added the words "suffering", "understanding" and "circle" to the justice train. Words, only, but damn, that invisible answer felt close.

From the style and angle of the carotid slash, he

knew without question that the same person who had murdered Luki Romero had also murdered Cori Baumgartner, Lionel Foret, Steve Oakland and back through Angel's favored soccer mom. Like the note, however, the pennies had been missing from Luki's eyelids and there'd been a number of post-death slices and stabs.

He'd seen that before, most notably in the case of the Boston cop. But why the seemingly random switch from neat to sloppy, from order to disorder, from calm to frantic?

An attempted cover-up? Definite possibility. Reason for the poor attempt? Could be a deliberate ploy but he doubted it. Undue haste seemed more likely. Ah, but then the kicker. Why only the occasional bad cover of a signature murder? He had no answer for that one. Yet.

Noah prowled through the condo. An hour bled into ninety minutes. He went through everything, from medicine cabinet to sock drawer to surgical files.

…And found it in a shoebox labeled "Tax Receipts", stuffed between a pair of four hundred-dollar debit slips that read "Business Dinner".

The take-out burger wrapper had been crumpled and smoothed several times. Even so, the stenciled words chilled.

THE CIRCLE CLOSES WITH AN ANGEL'S DEATH.
HE WHO SUFFERS LAST WILL UNDERSTAND AT LAST
AND WATCH ME SEAL THE CIRCLE.

Swearing, Noah launched out of the condo.

He was hunting for his cell phone when it rang. Caller unknown, he read as he ran down the stairs.

He answered with an impatient "Graydon." Then halted with his hand on the fire door as a distorted voice slithered into his ear.

"Come to Brogan's farm, Agent Graydon. Come and watch the woman you love die. If her cell phone rings, she's dead where she stands. Otherwise, I give you a small chance to save her." A ratchety laugh reached him. "Pray, Noah, that your Angel receives no calls..."

ANGEL PUSHED HER VEHICLE hard. The rain and darkness made driving treacherous, but at least she knew her destination.

Why Brogan's farm? she wondered as she navigated a series of hairpin turns. Because it was remote, obviously. And known to her. Also—and she'd checked this en route—tonight wasn't one of farmer Brogan's pumpkin smashing nights. He was playing poker with a neighbor. There'd be no one to watch the Penny Killer's bloodbath go down.

"Hell with that," she muttered to the darkness. It was the killer's time to go down. And he wouldn't be taking Noah with him.

Hobo's last words repeated to the slap of the windshield wipers. Rain pelted roof and hood. With each sound, she heard the killer's name, pictured his face.

She could see it all now. Graeme Thomas, saver of lives, scrabbling like a rat through human blood, stabbing and slashing and darting furtive looks over his shoulder. Get in, get out, mustn't get caught.

Hobo's description had been eerily perfect. The trench coat Graeme habitually wore, his dark, curling hair, slicked back to reveal a slight widow's peak. Wide mouth to accommodate his big smile. Tall, elegant—and out of his mind to be committing such brutal acts. "Damn you," she whispered. "If Noah's hurt again…"

No, she wouldn't go there. Couldn't. Instead, she pictured a jumble of other horrors—victims' faces, blood, pennies, a burning warehouse, more blood, a soccer ball, Lionel Foret's mother, Luki Romero's brother.

Oh yeah—brother of man. Stupid miss, there. She should have twigged to that reference much sooner. Except she'd been thinking in another direction, hadn't she? The wrong direction.

The entrance to the farm came up quickly. Angel braked for the turn. Her fingers itched to use her cell phone. She'd left a message earlier for Liz, but hadn't dared call Noah. Maybe the killer had been bluffing. But what if he hadn't?

Her heart shot into her throat when she spied Noah's truck in the muddy barnyard. Pieces of pumpkin littered the ground. Part of a hideous face leered up at her when she stepped out.

She tested her flashlight against her palm. The beam shone strong and steady. Gun ready, she started for the big door.

Mud squelched around her ankles. Her boots sank deeper with each step. The barn was the only place that made sense. Where else could she go but there?

No light burned in the windows. No sound emanated from inside. The creak of the ancient hinges doubled her heart rate. Then a blast of wet wind swooped down to shove her inside and the big door closed.

Now there was only a vast empty space, a ladder— and a loft.

Suddenly, there she was, six years old again, hidden behind a bale of hay, terrified of the creatures hobbling toward her, only slightly more terrified of the man below.

"Not now," she whispered and squashed the memory.

The cobwebbed loft ladder loomed ahead. Her flashlight showed something glinting dully on the fifth rung. Heart thumping, she made her way toward it.

Where were Noah and the killer? Yes, this was a trap. Accepted and dealt with. But why the game of hide and seek? And why… "Oh, hell." She breathed out. Why two pennies sitting side by side on the fifth rung?

Obviously, he wanted her in the loft.

She spotted the handkerchief next, tied to the top of the ladder.

"Yes, right, got that one," she murmured, and with an apprehensive upward look began to climb.

The sound of a protesting plank reached her above the wind that howled through the rafters. There was someone in the loft.

Trap, her brain repeated. With Noah quite possibly in the center of it.

Leaving the pennies, Angel finished the climb. She extinguished her light near the top. True, she couldn't see the killer. But he wouldn't see her either, and even sightless, she had to be the better shot.

The floor gave when she stepped from the ladder. She heard a thud, and another. Soft but audible.

"Noah?" she called into the gloom. Then side-stepped, just in case.

Two more tiny thumps preceded a double squeak. Could it get any creepier? Angel debated for a moment, finally switched on her light.

The eyes appeared red at first, round gleaming orbs, staring with an expression of malicious glee—as a trio of bats limped toward her on the tips of their folded wings.

Chapter Sixteen

She didn't scream, didn't make a sound, but the sight of the bats momentarily paralyzed her. When a pair of hands wrapped around her upper arms, she snapped back, reacting as she'd been trained to by one of the FBI's best.

"Angel, it's me." Noah's voice in her ear stopped her elbow half an inch below his jaw.

Stressed to the max, she jerked free. Then she remembered her earlier terror and took his face in her hands. "He said he had you." She peppered his mouth and cheeks with kisses. "He told me…" The second memory struck, and she jumped back. "Oh, damn, hell, yuck—bats—on the floor."

He let her drag him sideways, toward the edge. "Angel, they can't…"

"Where are they? Where's he?" She searched the blackened rafters. "He put them here to scare me. He knows I'm terrified of them. Where are they?"

"Angel, calm down."

"I am calm." She breathed carefully, tried to recall where the ladder was without resorting to her light. "If I was truly panicking, I'd be lying in a heap on the floor by now." She raised her eyes to the rafters. "Probably what he wants. But you're safe. You're alive." She hugged him again, kissed his neck. "Thank God he didn't hurt you." She felt his ribs. "He didn't, did he?"

"I'm fine."

And holding her, Angel suddenly realized, in a grip King Kong would have envied.

"Uh, Noah, I can't breathe."

"Bats can't hurt you. The Penny Killer can."

"Still can't breathe." She twisted until he relaxed his arm muscles.

With her eyes on the spot where she'd sighted the bats, she asked, "Is he here? Have you seen him?"

"Yes, he's here—stop backing up; I won't let them near you—but no, I haven't seen him."

"Great, now we play ga—ames. Whoa!"

Despite Noah's promise, she'd continued to edge backward. Now she had to cling to him for support as her right foot encountered only air. "Sorry, I know, just bats. No match for a killer on the danger scale." Or so she'd tell herself until she believed. "Is he playing us as a pair?"

"Oh, yeah."

"You sound very definite. Why?"

"I went to Graeme's condo on a hunch."

"If you want to explain that answer, it might be easier for me to forget about the—" she shuddered, searched for the ladder with her foot "—you know."

"I found a second note inside."

"And it said?" She located the top rung, offered a prayer of thanks.

"It's not what it said that matters, it's that it was there at all."

"You could be a little clearer, Noah."

"Later. For now, let's get the hell out of here—if we can."

Didn't seem likely, but Angel was more than happy to make the attempt.

Until she stepped on the first rung.

She felt Noah stop, felt his body stiffen and shift. "Go," he said in an undertone.

Angel's head came up as a light flared beside her. She didn't want to look, didn't want to see ugly reality. But he gave her no choice.

"Turn your pretty head, Angel, and look at me. Know who I am."

The face that seemed to float beyond Noah's shoulder was familiar, yet oddly grotesque. For him, the shadows didn't flatter.

"So here we all are," the Penny Killer said. His lips stretched into a lurid smile. "Cooperate, Angel, and I'll let your lover live. You have my word on that. And mine is a word you can take to the grave."

SHE'D NEVER WANTED anything to be a nightmare so badly in her life. Even her fear of bats paled by comparison.

The killer's face went from smiling to sorrowful. "You're disappointed. Did you guess, or is the shock in the reveal? Guns down, people." He gestured. "On the floor below. Lose them, or you're dead, one, two. I've got a half-squeezed trigger aimed at your spinal column, Noah, and, guess what? Several evenings last summer when I should have been at the Support Center, I fibbed and said I had to work so I could go off and shoot targets."

Noah gave Angel a small nod. She followed his lead and tossed her gun to the lower level.

"Very good, now turn around. Slowly." He motioned with his gun, an FBI special, Angel noted. "Separate. Angel, go left, Noah, right. Should probably watch out for falling bats, Angel." He bent closer to stage-whisper. "They're waking up."

It was as much as she could manage, but no way would she give him any more satisfaction than he'd already taken from the situation. She worked up a smile. "You've been doing target practice, and I've been working on my fear factor." Shrugging, she jammed her hands into her jacket pockets. "We all have our demons. Apparently yours won the war a long time ago."

Unruffled, he circled away from them. "You

can't goad me, Angel. I'm not built that way. My anger, my resentment, my contempt are deep-rooted. They go all the way back to my childhood. Did you know my grandmother was killed by a drunk driver after an office party? No? The judge in the case was sympathetic to the driver. More correctly, he bought her sob story. Or was blinded by her spectacular breasts. Whatever the case, she got a slap on the wrist. Couldn't drive for a whole year. And, oh yeah, a month's wages went toward her fine. She was and still is the CEO of a large shoe company. Ironic, isn't it, that those boots you're wearing tonight could very well come from one of her company's factories. Noah's—mmm—not so much."

He waved his weapon. "Nothing to say, Noah? No wherefores or whys? Come on, you must have a million 'why' questions. Why you and Angel? Why now? Why the others? Why the long break? Still nothing, huh? Okay, how about: When did I start? What made me start? Well, actually I answered that one, but I can give you another personal example for interest's sake.

"My cousin, who's a great guy, got shafted during his divorce, thanks largely to his ex's scummy lawyer. Did the lawyer give a rat's ass that my cousin had every right to his fifty percent share of the couple's mutual holdings? No, the high-priced slime bag worked it down to ninety-ten. His ex even got the dog. My cousin wound up living in a dive. Lost his job and a lot of his friends. He offed himself two years later."

Keeping her hands in her pockets, Angel used the speed dial on her cell phone.

"You know, you two are really dull." The killer paced two steps left, four right. "Don't you have anything to say or ask? You were chatty enough before I stepped out and did the 'Here I am, it's me' thing…Noah?"

"Figured it out before I got here."

"Not sure I buy that. When? How?"

"Tonight, but I think suspicion's been building since Luki Romero died."

"Huh." He turned to Angel. "What about you?"

A chill feathered along her spine as a gust of wind moaned in the high rafters. "No suspicion. I talked to a man who witnessed the last murder. He gave me a description, and suddenly it all made horrible sense. But why Brogan's farm? And why us—me?"

"Guess it didn't all make sense, huh?" His smile was a hideous parody of the one she knew. His wink only made the weight in her chest that much heavier. "Bet Noah could tell you. Shall we ask him, or would you rather die in ignorance? Because I can close the circle any time now… Oh, don't give me that look, Noah. I realize if I take the time to slice her carotid I'll be dead before she is. But hey there, people, the statement I've been attempting to make from the start has been screwed up so many times, it doesn't matter anymore how you die. Cut, shot, pushed from this loft, it's all the same in the end. Wouldn't have been once, but now dead'll do just fine. Circle closed, circle sealed. And only one of us walks away." The shadows transformed his face into an evil mask. "Any guesses," he asked, "as to who the walker will be?" He made a summoning motion with his fingers. "Come on, Noah. You've got a fifty-fifty shot at this one. You or me, who's it gonna be?"

Ignoring the terror that crawled through her like an army of red ants, Angel gave into her disgust. "You think this is funny, some kind of game we're playing?"

That did it. He whipped the gun up, stiff-armed, pointed it at her face. His features lost all trace of jocularity. "You want serious, Angel, you want mad? I'll give you fury. A truckload of it."

The change was so abrupt, so complete that Angel's breath quite literally stalled in her chest. Was she crazy? Challenging a lunatic with a gun? She needed a serious refresher course in situation management.

Fortunately, Noah didn't. "Answer's me," he said in a level tone. The killer swung his gun sharply sideways. "I'm the one who'll walk. Angel dies because of me—circle closed. Then you take your own life—circle sealed. Payback, possibly, for all the lives you've taken."

"Is that what you think?"

Noah moved a shoulder. "Judge Baumgartner let a killer go free. People suffered because of his decision. Sure, other people died, but those aren't the ones you're standing for, is it? You represent the victims' families, their friends, their lovers. The survivors. They grieve, you avenge. Baumgartner caused families to grieve; now he's grieving himself."

Rain drummed angry fists on the roof and walls as Angel picked up the thread. "It's all about justice, isn't it? The soccer mom didn't do anything wrong, but three months before she died, her husband, a computer geek with his own business, refused to let a woman into his shop, even though she was banging on his door, screaming that her boyfriend was trying to kill her."

"Wouldn't let her in and didn't even bother to call the cops," the killer retorted. "He just checked the bars on his shop window and scuttled into the back room. Result? The woman's boyfriend killed her."

"But the guy with the shop admitted later…"

"What? That, oh yeah, guess maybe I should have phoned the police, but ooh, I was scared, wasn't thinking straight. Yeah, he was so scared, he went straight back to his online poker game and his beer. The woman who died had three kids. So did he. Ta-da! See how it feels, geek, to lose your spouse… And you can just stop right there with the looks," he snapped when Noah shifted position.

"You screwed up, too. Big time. So climb down from your high horse, and accept the consequences of your own actions instead of judging mine."

Noah glanced at Angel, made a barely perceptible head motion. "Jerry Kraus?"

"Got it in one."

Very carefully, Angel widened the gap between them. "Noah wasn't the only person who vouched for Kraus," she said, for no other reason than getting the killer's attention shifted, allowing Noah to broaden the gap a little more. "But then I suppose that's why Steve Oakland's dead, isn't it? You discovered he was Brian Pinkney's son. Like Noah, Brian stood up for Kraus at the FBI hearing."

"Exactly right. At long last, Angel, you've got it." His mouth turned down as if dragged by an elastic. "I don't enjoy killing, you know. It goes against my personal values, and my professional ethics. But the chaos these so-called good people create needs to be put right. You've heard the story about Lionel Foret's mother? Two teenagers died as a result of her interference. Directly because of it. Well, now her kid's dead. Tit for tat, Ms. Foret-Smith."

"And Luki Romero," Noah said above the shrieking wind. "Dead because of his brother?"

"Man's a killer."

Another vague half smile as Noah looked past him and into the deeper shadows. "That would be your so-called pot-kettle scenario, wouldn't it?" He brought his gaze back, gave Angel the opportunity to edge another few steps to the side. "You're not planning to kill yourself because of the murders you've committed. You're doing it to make someone pay. That's the deal, isn't it? When you die, Liz will be left with a history she'll never be able to live down. All mistakes finally paid for in full. Five long years of waiting, and tonight it's done. Isn't it, Joe?"

Chapter Seventeen

Joe's features confirmed everything Noah had said. Angel watched his expression go from angry to anguished to appreciative, and saw, possibly for the first time in her career, the true face of insanity.

She wondered which was stronger, his hatred for Noah, or the contempt he felt for his wife. Wondered, but knew better than to ask.

Eyes lit with anticipation, Joe took a menacing step forward. "At last, the brilliance emerges. And here I was beginning to doubt you. The great Noah Graydon. I assume you know Pretender Pete's real name by now."

Noah gave him nothing back by way of emotion. "Yeah, I know it," he said simply. "Doesn't matter. He stole another man's identity so he could start a new life. The real Pete was dead. Our Pete made the discovery, made the decision, made the switch. He'd done his time in prison, now suddenly, there it was, his chance to start a new life."

"Yes, but going back—and even overlooking the

fact that he left a dead man to rot as I learned by a clever spate of eavesdropping—there's still the little matter of that crime to which you alluded and for which he supposedly paid. It's called murder, folks."

"It was deemed an accidental death." Noah's gaze didn't waver. "The Pete we know served eight years before his parole."

"Then he jumped parole, stole the identity of a dead man and opened a restaurant on the other side of the country where, what a coincidence, his ex-wife just happened to be living. Ex-wife who never mentioned first husband to second, I might add. There she was, remarried, happy, with two kids and her ever-loving, totally oblivious hubby. So what does happy wifey do? She sneaks around behind hubby's back with her parole-jumping, identity-thief ex. Did you know that the guy Pretender Pete killed in the heat of an argument over—God help me here—a slut named Ruby, had a brother, a sister and two very nice parents? Pretender Pete's victim was also a counselor at AA. That's how he met Ruby. Counselor liked her, they started dating. Then along came good old Pete with his big laugh and his thick curly hair. The affair was inevitable, right? So was the fistfight—which our Pete won, no problem. Oh, but there was a problem, because the last punch he threw knocked the counselor to the ground where he hit his head on a pointy rock. End of AA counselor. Manslaughter charge for Pretender Pete.

"Eight years later, Pete's out and itching to get on with life. The counselor's family takes flowers to his grave every Sunday afternoon at three o'clock, while Liz helps his killer, her ex, do God knows what behind her second husband's back." He spun. "What do you think of that tale, Angel? Should we give it to Paul Reuben to print?"

Joe turned so fast, he almost caught her edging sideways. She compensated by pretending to search for bats. "Maybe she's been trying to talk Pete into turning himself in."

"Dear Lord, were you born an idealist?"

"You asked me what I thought. That's it."

"Even if you're right, it doesn't alter the fact that she's been helping a man that murdered a man who left a loving family behind. Or that she lied by omission about being married to him. Well, tough for her, Angel face." The click of his gun echoed through the barn in spite of the storm. "Because Noah was dead on. Liz is going to know firsthand how it feels to be left behind. To be alone. To suffer."

Wind raged against the barn's weathered outer walls. Rain lashed the north side, the door side. Angel fingered her cell phone and continued to offer up silent prayers.

"It ends tonight," Joe told them. "Done, finished, finally." He gave a dry-as-dust laugh. "It's taken me years to get here, Noah, to find a way to make you pay. The ultimate loner. Loved his parents, yes, but those parents are dead. There were women, of course, few men would choose to be that alone, but none who ever got into your head, or your heart. I dealt with Brian way back when, but you… Who could I remove from your life to make you grieve?

"Then it happened. Three and half years after Oakland's death you started having conversations with a woman. Six months passed, and I began to wonder. Maybe there's something here. Another year crept by. Oh, yeah, he cares. Then you met. And fell. Now it's love all around. Don't insult me by denying it. You love, you lose. You understand. It's how I get the people I kill to come to me. Love is, as they say, the universal key. Threaten a true loved one and most people will do anything, go anywhere. It's a handy little emotion, don't you agree?"

"Joe, stop," Angel tried. "You know you need help. Please, please don't do this."

But the man she'd known since coming to Boston merely chuckled. "Forget it, Angel. No need to placate or plead with the crazy man. No need and no point. I've had a goal from the start. Justice for those who are left behind, Luki Romero both excepted and included. I got a twofer with him. Scum with no record gone. Scum with record hurts. What could be better?"

"Much better, if you put the gun down and let Angel and Noah go," a new voice inserted.

Angel brought her head around, but beyond that and a quick eye flick in Noah's direction, didn't move. Didn't breathe as Liz finished climbing the ladder. And stepped off to face her husband.

SHE HADN'T EXPECTED HER partner to rush in without backup, or she would never have left a message on her voice mail earlier. She certainly wouldn't have speed dialed her cell in the hopes that Liz would pick up and hear what was happening in the loft.

"Joe, please." Liz took a placating step forward. "Don't…"

The shot rang out. The bullet caught her mid torso, just to the left of her stomach. Shock registered as she extended a hand toward the gun.

It was all the diversion Noah needed. He moved so fast, Angel missed the actual motion. She would have followed him without a second thought if Liz hadn't crumpled to the floor.

Reacting quickly, she caught her friend by the shoulders, set her back against the wall, then untied Joe's handkerchief from the ladder and used it to stem the blood flow.

The bullet had gone in deep, she realized. Liz needed help, fast. With a fearful glance into the shadows, she used her cell to call 911.

"Paramedics are coming," she said and adjusted the handkerchief. "Hold on, Liz, just please, hold on."

Imploring fingers snared her wrist. "Don't let

him kill you, or Noah. Use my gun… Stop him, Angel."

"Do my best."

She dragged the gun from Liz's holster, pivoted. Joe was there, directly in front of her and in her sights. Noah had managed to kick his weapon aside. She took aim. But then Joe's arm hit the kerosene lamp and knocked it sideways. When it fell, the loft went dark… For about two seconds.

The base landed on a shallow bed of straw. Fed by the kerosene, flames shot across the planks.

Liz struggled out of her coat. "I'll try to smother it. Help Noah."

With a brief hesitation for her friend's condition, Angel focused on the sounds across the loft.

Joe grunted, snarled, swore. Beside her, the flames raced toward an old post and rocketed upward. She heard wings and frantic squeals, felt something brush her cheek. She wanted to scream but swallowed it and called Noah's name.

She could almost see him, could certainly tell the difference between the two men. But they kept moving, up and down, left and right, forward and backward. Targeting Joe alone was impossible.

Smoke began to fill the loft. Wings flapped everywhere. Angel spied a boarded up window and, running to it, used her foot to kick the shutter loose. Then she ducked as every winged creature in the barn flew toward it.

Low to the ground, she adjusted her grip on

Liz's gun. Where were they? She could hear them but could no longer see through the smoke.

She spied Noah, just for an instant. Then he vanished and Joe appeared.

Angel didn't hesitate, even when a leathery wing tangled itself in her hair. She aimed, fired—and heard a growl of pain.

Please God, not Noah.

Smoke billowed and swirled. The fire leaped from post to rafter, spreading outward like a paper fan.

Bits of charred wood dropped to the floor. The embers sparked a whole new series of fires.

Through the flames, Angel spotted Joe's knife. She grabbed it with her left hand.

Coughing, Liz fell on her from behind. "Tell Noah Joe's peripheral vision's bad, really bad… Left eye. Come at him that way."

Angel relayed the message, fought to balance herself and her partner.

"Got to get out," Liz panted. "Smoke'll kill us."

Disentangling, Angel propelled her toward the ladder. "I won't leave Noah. Can you make it down alone?"

"No. Angel don't…"

"Have to. Love him. Go."

Angel waved at the choking smoke, breathed into the crook of her arm.

A fist struck flesh. And again. Joe stumbled into her line of vision. She still had the knife. When he lunged for it, she snatched it out of reach. Then tripped and went down.

He showed his teeth in a freakish caricature of a smile. "One way or another," he shouted and threw himself on her. "We die!"

"Like hell we do," she shot back. But when he landed and they rolled, her arm collided with one of the smoldering posts, and the blackened wood sizzled the flesh on her wrist. She hissed in a breath, dropped the knife.

"Time to die." Teeth bared, Joe reared back, holding the recaptured knife in his right hand.

Unable to free herself, Angel used her elbow on his crotch. She saw his eyes widen, then, oddly, begin to cloud.

"Circle's not complete," he whispered. A slow hiss of air emerged. "Damn you, Noah, she's not..."

His eyes widened slightly, then went glassy. Blood appeared at the corners of his mouth. His jaw dropped as he collapsed onto the right side of Angel's body.

He was dead weight on top of her. Truly dead weight. His glasses dug into her throat. The knife lay inches from his outstretched fingers.

Angel pushed and squirmed. She saw the dead bat she'd tripped on and shivered in spite of herself. Then suddenly, Joe's body vanished, and Noah was kneeling beside her, breathing hard and—

"Oh my God, you're bleeding." Mindless of the smoke and flames, she scrambled up, tore at his T.

"It's nothing." Catching her hand, he pulled her to her feet. "Joe got hold of a pitchfork. One of the prongs caught me. Lucky shot." With his good arm Noah hauled her up against him, kissed her, then pushed. "Go. Now."

"But…"

"Get out of here, Angel. Help Liz. I'll get Joe."

The smoke was too thick for her to argue, and portions of the roof were beginning to shower down.

Even so, she waited until Noah dragged Joe's body to the ladder. Then she sucked in as much air as she could and climbed down.

She spotted Liz half conscious and mumbling, huddled next to an empty feed bin.

"Not gonna make it," her friend predicted in a slur. "Joe?"

"Noah's got him." Taking her partner by the arms, Angel tugged with gentle urgency. The smoke was so dense now, she could hardly see the floor. She coughed to clear her lungs. "We have to get out."

"But Joe…"

"Liz, he's dead." She coughed again. "And we'll be joining him if we don't leave now." She waved at the smoke, raised her voice. "Noah?"

He appeared beside her. "Out, Angel. I'm right behind you."

What choice did she have?

Hungry flames had already crawled down the

lower walls. Somehow—and the memory was little more than a blur, Angel half shoved, half carried Liz through the door.

The rain on her face was a cold but welcome slap. Angel limped Liz to her car and sat her down with care. She recalled that the emergency kit was in the trunk and staggered to her feet.

She called to Noah, but the wind drove her words straight back at her. Then she saw him, and her eyes closed briefly as her throat filled with too many emotions to separate.

He laid Joe down next to his truck, went to one knee for a moment, then stood and caught her eye. A second later, one of the shadows to his left came to life and jumped him.

Chapter Eighteen

"You killed my brother! You murdered him! He was sick, and you put a bullet in his skull!"

Graeme raged at them, at him, Noah reflected, for close to an hour. The paramedics gave him a sedative as soon as they arrived, but its effect was negligible. Graeme alternated between straining to view his brother's body and doing his utmost to reach Noah again.

Detaching him after the initial attack had been easy enough with Angel's help. Tiger protecting a cub, Noah recalled, and smiled a little at the memory. She'd have kicked Graeme's butt back to Boston if he hadn't blocked the attempt and steered her over to her partner.

Would Liz survive? Angel and the paramedics said yes. Liz said nothing.

The police arrival was followed by a carload of feds. Graeme was further sedated and strapped to a gurney for his ride to the hospital. Angel dealt with her boss's jackass of an assistant, while Brian

Pinkney circled Joe's still, prone body like a satisfied vulture.

Noah had nothing to say to the man, and evidently Brian felt the same. Never had been, never would be friends. But at least now it was done. Some might call that closure. The end of a nightmare was all Noah saw.

Twenty minutes later, Angel scraped off Bergman's sniveling assistant and with a brief detour to view the corpse, she set her sights on the tractor where Noah had hoisted himself to observe and reflect.

"Needed to look at him again, huh?" he asked as she approached.

"Something like that." The rain had slowed to a drizzle, and she shoved the wet hair from her face. "I put the pennies he left inside on his eyelids. I think they're for the ferryman. So does Graeme."

"You talked to Graeme?"

"He had a few lucid moments before the ambulance left. The ferryman's part of an ancient Greek myth. He takes dead people, good and bad, to the other side. The coins pay for passage. Either that or Joe was making a psychological statement about people not being able to see what's directly in front of them because they're blinded by—well, things. They lose the ability to distinguish right from wrong, can't or won't see the harm that could result from their actions."

Hopping down and careful not to jar his injured

shoulder, Noah drew her into his arms, turned his face into her hair. "You after my job, Angel?"

"After something," she agreed. "We lost a friend tonight, Noah. At least we thought he was a friend. I should feel terrible, but all I feel right now is empty."

"It'll pass." As flames continued to crackle behind him, Noah looked beyond her to Joe's prone body. "When it does, trust me, it'll hurt like hell. Joe was one of the first people I met in Boston. He was single and quiet, liked the Celtics, home-brewed beer and chess. He met and married Liz right after he killed Steve Oakland."

"Then five years passed, Liz got tangled up with her ex-husband, and the killing started again. Coincidence?"

Noah shook his head. "For the stopping, maybe. Not for the restart. That was me. He had an old score to settle, and my feelings for you gave him the opportunity to do it."

"Okay, stop right there." Pushing back, Angel caught his face in her hands. "I mean it. Just stop. What Joe did isn't your fault. You're not responsible for his actions."

"I was his friend, Angel. I should have seen what he was, what he was doing."

"So should I. So should Liz. So should Graeme. Well, actually…" She rocked her head. "Graeme did see, but that's a separate issue. I had dinners at Joe and Liz's place, lots of them. Liz was married to the man." She tapped her temple. "Missed it, both of us. Graeme was the only one who twigged, and let's face it, he didn't exactly deal in the best possible way. I know he loved Joe, but to cover up murder after murder for him? Makes him a monster after the fact."

"It also accounts for the discrepancies in MO."

"Brother of man," she recalled. "We thought the reference related to Joe, but that note we found in Graeme's pocket wasn't his. Graeme took it from Luki Romero while he was maiming the guy's body. Sammi would suffer because of Luki's death."

She didn't argue or struggle when Noah turned her around and lifted her onto the tractor seat. She merely asked, "You said you found a second note at Graeme's place. What was that all about?"

"Joe wrote it for himself, an allusion to his own death. He planned to close the circle of revenge with your death and seal it with his own. He said it himself, he wanted Liz to suffer for helping a murderer—her ex-husband—and so she would, through her current husband's death."

"You don't think he was paying himself back in some small way for the murders he'd committed?"

"To some extent, possibly. In any case, Graeme got hold of the note and hid it in his condo. I imagine he knew what Joe was planning to do. The question was, could he stop him from doing it?"

"Unlikely," Angel predicted. "What was the deal

with the candy wrappers and napkins Joe used as
note paper?"

"Just another statement. Through acts that had
little or no effect on the perpetrators, innocent
people became victims. Joe saw them all the time
at the Support Center. Grieving friends and
families, put in that position by people like Joy
Foret Smith and Judge Baumgartner. Toss-off
actions equaled toss-off notes. Or something like
that."

"As always, Graydon, I'm impressed." She
rested her forehead against his. "Hobo described
Graeme perfectly. He didn't get a clear look at the
killer, but he saw Graeme rush in less than a minute
after Joe left. Fortunately, Paul was there, too, at
the top of the alley, so as much as he wanted to,
Graeme couldn't do anything to Cori Baumgartner's body. He could only pick up the handkerchief
Joe had dropped and run. Hobo waited until
Graeme was gone, dumped Cori's purse and stole
her wallet. Unfortunately, that left Paul, Joe's
media connection to a highly confused world,
behind as lone suspect. I assume Joe wanted said
connection to see one of the murders firsthand.
Unless, of course, he was trying to set Paul up, buy
some time…" She sighed. "Are you as lost as I
am?"

"Not quite. Paul was a tool, plain and simple. Joe
had a point to make. We might have figured it out
sooner if his brother hadn't been trying to protect

him. Graeme's interference explains why Luki Romero's death didn't fit the mold. Ditto the cop and the marketing director from the past."

"Wherever, whenever opportunity strikes." Lifting her head, Angel followed Noah's gaze to the sea of red fire trucks. "I feel so incredibly sad, or will when I can feel anything again. Graeme did what he did out of love for his brother. God knows how many charges he'll face by tomorrow. On the other side, Liz knew, or rather discovered, that her ex-husband was an identity thief."

"When did she figure it out?"

"She says just after Halloween, right around the time of Foret's murder. She knew he was in Boston, obviously, but that was easy enough to deal with. They could pretend they'd just met, no mention of a past relationship. But then Pete came to her and admitted the name he'd been using belonged to a dead man. Accidentally dead, he insisted, not murdered. Until then, Liz assumed he'd changed his name in the usual way. You know the deal, fresh out of prison, gonna start a new life. Except he didn't do it quite the way he'd led her to believe. Joe was right about Pretender Pete jumping parole. Okay, maybe Liz should have gone into the records and checked out the conditions of that parole, but she didn't. Long story short, when she realized what he'd done, she pushed him to turn himself in. Not sure how Bergman'll take the story, but we'll find out soon enough. FYI, she married Pete when she was seventeen, and divorced him a year later."

A smile grazed Noah's lips. "You're just full of information, aren't you?"

"Energy's coming back in spurts. Hopefully, emotion won't be far behind."

The smile deepened. "Sounds promising, all things considered." Running his thumb lightly over her chin, he drew her forward. He also drew a shiver. Even more promising. "His name's Harry John Crooke."

"Seriously?" She ran it through her head. "When the horror's over and before he's old and gray, Harry might want to think about changing that surname. Legally this time."

"Yeah, well, he's got a few other problems to sort out first."

Angel wrapped a finger around his hair, tugged. "I guess that's what life's all about, huh? Making choices, making decisions, dealing with stress, accepting what you can't change…"

"Changing what you can."

She gave a harder tug. "Hey, half the people I deal with have gone through some kind of twelve-step program, Graydon. Most of the other half could use one." Concern clouded her eyes. "Do you think Liz'll be all right? She looked so—I don't know—vacant when she left here."

"She'll survive," Noah said. "Tonight, because she has to. Eventually, because she'll want to. She has kids, she has family, she has friends. She'll borrow whatever strength she can't find inside herself."

"Is that what you did?"

"No." He skimmed a knuckle along her throat to her collarbone. "That was my mistake. I thought alone was better. Safer. Can't get hurt if you don't get close. After my run-in with the Penny Killer, I withdrew even more. Not smart, not healthy. Not for anyone. You could have been killed, Angel, because of me."

She tapped a finger to his chin. "But I wasn't killed, was I? Because of you. Depends how you say it, Noah. I'll go with the positive spin every time. Try it, you might just get hooked." Her eyes began to dance. "How would you like to meet my mother?"

He stared, almost laughed. "What?"

"She's really nice, has a great Harley and a super-cool boyfriend. They're coming to Boston for Thanksgiving. Face it, Graydon, as bad as it's been, we have a lot to be thankful for."

"Yeah, we're alive."

"Oh, I think you can do better than that." She fingered his bandaged shoulder through his jacket. "The Penny Killer's gone. Okay, the solution was sad, and we'll have to work our way through that, but Liz is alive, and Pete, sorry, Harry, didn't murder his namesake, so that's good. And here's a work-related bonus. Bergman's assistant is being transferred to New York. I'd celebrate if I thought this energy stream was going to last. Unfortunately, when it fades, I'm likely to fall asleep wherever I happen to be."

Noah ran a hand around the back of her neck. "Then you should be home."

"I'm game if you are." She held his gaze, wouldn't let him look away. "Did I mention that I love you?"

Emotions so strong he almost didn't recognize them gathered in his chest. Had, he suspected, been gathering since the first time they'd spoken on the phone.

Gently trapping her jaw between his fingers and thumb, he held her still for his kiss. When he lifted his head several seconds later, he murmured a quiet, "I love you, too, Angel. I think it's time I showed you just how much."

"You mean I can…?"

He dropped his hands, held them out to the sides. "If you want to."

He let her give him a deep bolstering kiss, then watched her face as she raised the patch over his left eye.

And fell in love all over again when a soft, slow smile stole across her lips.

* * * * *

*Celebrate 60 years of pure reading pleasure
with Harlequin® Books!*

*Harlequin Romance® is celebrating by
showering you with DIAMOND BRIDES
in February, 2009.
Six stories that promise to bring a touch of
sparkle to your life, with diamond proposals and
dazzling weddings, sparkling brides
and gorgeous grooms!*

*Enjoy a sneak peek at Caroline Anderson's
TWO LITTLE MIRACLES,
available February 2009
from Harlequin Romance®.*

"I'VE FOUND HER."

Max froze.

It was what he'd been waiting for since June, but now—now he was almost afraid to voice the question. His heart stalling, he leaned slowly back in his chair and scoured the investigator's face for clues. "Where?" he asked, and his voice sounded rough and unused, like a rusty hinge.

"In Suffolk. She's living in a cottage."

Living. His heart crashed back to life, and he sucked in a long, slow breath. All these months he'd feared—

"Is she well?"

"Yes, she's well."

He had to force himself to ask the next question. "Alone?"

The man paused. "No. The cottage belongs to a man called John Blake. He's working away at the moment, but he comes and goes."

God. He felt sick. So sick he hardly registered

the next few words, but then gradually they sank in. "She's got *what?*"

"Babies. Twin girls. They're eight months old."

"Eight—?" he echoed under his breath. "They must be his."

He was thinking out loud, but the P.I. heard and corrected him.

"Apparently not. I gather they're hers. She's been there since mid-January last year, and they were born during the summer—June, the woman in the post office thought. She was more than helpful. I think there's been a certain amount of speculation about their relationship."

He'd just bet there had. God, he was going to kill her. Or Blake. Maybe both of them.

"Of course, looking at the dates, she was presumably pregnant when she left you, so they could be yours, or she could have been having an affair with this Blake character before…"

He glared at the unfortunate P.I. "Just stick to your job. I can do the math," he snapped, swallowing the unpalatable possibility that she'd been unfaithful to him before she'd left. "Where is she? I want the address."

"It's all in here," the man said, sliding a large envelope across the desk to him. "With my invoice."

"I'll get it seen to. Thank you."

"If there's anything else you need, Mr. Gallagher, any further information—"

"I'll be in touch."

"The woman in the post office told me Blake was away at the moment, if that helps," he added quietly, and opened the door.

Max stared down at the envelope, hardly daring to open it, but when the door clicked softly shut behind the P.I., he eased up the flap, tipped it and felt his breath jam in his throat as the photos spilled out over the desk.

Oh, lord, she looked gorgeous. Different, though. It took him a moment to recognize her, because she'd grown her hair, and it was tied back in a ponytail, making her look younger and somehow freer. The blond highlights were gone, and it was back to its natural soft golden-brown, with a little curl in the end of the ponytail that he wanted to thread his finger through and tug, just gently, to draw her back to him.

Crazy. She'd put on a little weight, but it suited her. She looked well and happy and beautiful, but oddly, considering how desperate he'd been for news of her for the past year—one year, three weeks and two days, to be exact—it wasn't only Julia who held his attention after the initial shock. It was the babies sitting side by side in a supermarket trolley. Two identical and absolutely beautiful little girls.

* * * * *

When Max Gallagher hires a P.I. to find his estranged wife, Julia, he discovers she's not alone—she has twin baby girls, and they might be his. Now workaholic Max has just two weeks to prove that he can be a wonderful husband and father to the family he wants to treasure.

Look for TWO LITTLE MIRACLES
by Caroline Anderson,
available February 2009
from Harlequin Romance®.

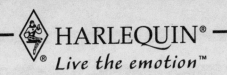

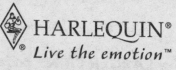

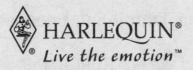

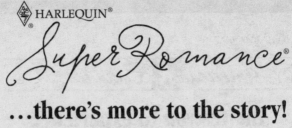

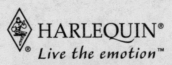

HARLEQUIN®
Presents®

The world's bestselling romance series...
The series that brings you your favorite authors,
month after month:

Helen Bianchin...Emma Darcy
Lynne Graham...Penny Jordan
Miranda Lee...Sandra Marton
Anne Mather...Carole Mortimer
Melanie Milburne...Michelle Reid

and many more talented authors!

Wealthy, powerful, gorgeous men...
Women who have feelings just like your own...
The stories you love, set in exotic, glamorous locations...

HARLEQUIN®
Presents®

Seduction and Passion Guaranteed!

Harlequin® Historical
Historical Romantic Adventure!

*Imagine a time of chivalrous
knights and unconventional ladies,
roguish rakes and impetuous
heiresses, rugged cowboys
and spirited frontierswomen—
these rich and vivid tales will
capture your imagination!*

*Harlequin Historical . . .
they're too good to miss!*

HHDIR06

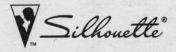

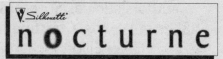

SPECIAL EDITION™

Emotional, compelling stories that capture the intensity of living, loving and creating a family in today's world.

Desire

Modern, passionate reads that are powerful and provocative.

nocturne

Dramatic and sensual tales of paranormal romance.

Romantic SUSPENSE

Romances that are sparked by danger and fueled by passion.